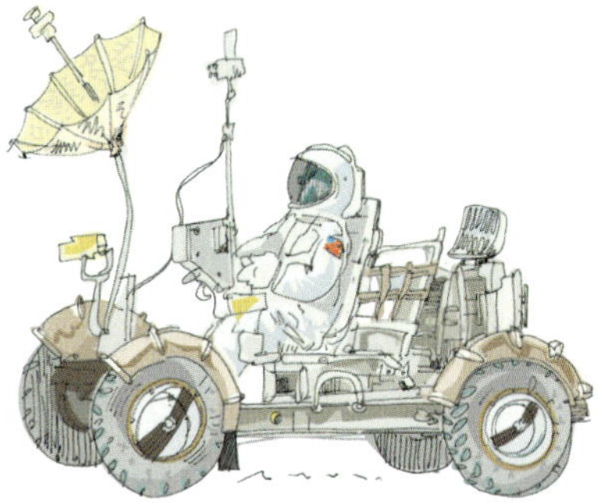

First published in Great Britain 2026 by Farshore
An imprint of HarperCollins*Publishers*
1 London Bridge Street, London SE1 9GF
www.farshore.co.uk

HarperCollins*Publishers*
Macken House, 39/40 Mayor Street Upper, Dublin 1, D01 C9W8, Ireland

Written by Dr Anne Rooney
Images used under license from
Shutterstock.com
Alamy.com
with additional images from
© NASA.gov – pages 6-9, 12-13, 16-17, 26-35, 38-39, 42-43, 46-47, 50-51, 58-63,
© Board of Trustees of the Science Museum – page 5, 68-69,
© Barry MacDonald – pages 14, 28-29, 36-37, 64-65,
© Ellie Pinney – page 44,
© Wikipedia Commons – page 39,
© Flickr.com – pages 32-33.

Produced under license for SCMG Enterprises Ltd. Science Museum® SCMG
Every purchase supports the museum. www.sciencemuseum.org.uk

ISBN 978 0 00 870573 2
Printed and bound in Romania
001

Adult supervision is advised for all craft and colouring activities.
Always ask an adult to help when using glue, paint and scissors.
Wear protective clothing and cover surfaces to avoid staining.
Adult supervision is always necessary when a child is cooking or using sharp implements.

A CIP catalogue record for this title is available from the British Library.

FSC
www.fsc.org
MIX
Paper | Supporting responsible forestry
FSC® C005461

SCIENCE MUSEUM

THIS ANNUAL BELONGS TO:

....

MY FAVOURITE PLANET IS:

....

CONTENTS

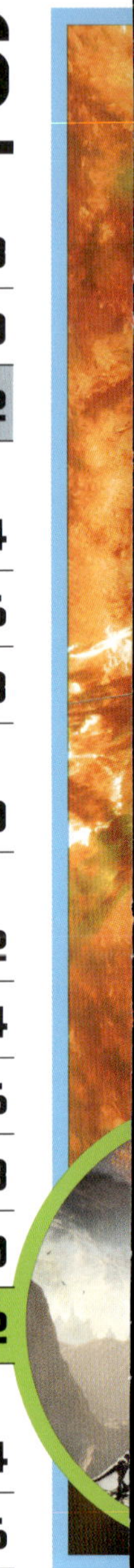

SCIENCE MUSEUM

Your base: Planet Earth

Our home planet is a great starting point for exploring space.

You are here!

Earth is a rocky planet in the Solar System – the collection of planets, moons and other objects orbiting the Sun, our local star. Earth is just right for us. It's not too hot or too cold, it has plenty of water, land to live on, and air we can breathe. Not everywhere is as welcoming.

Building a home

Our Solar System is about 4.5 billion years old. It began as a vast disc of dust, ice and gas whirling in space. The Sun formed from gas in the middle, and other bits stuck together, growing into planets, moons, comets and asteroids around it.

Around and around

Earth and the other planets orbit around the Sun. Earth takes 365 days to go round it once, making a year. And Earth itself rotates once every 24 hours, making a day. It's light when your bit of Earth faces the Sun and dark (night) when it faces out into space.

Hot or cold?

Earth doesn't stand straight up, but tilts on its axis. For part of the year the northern hemisphere is tipped towards the Sun and has longer daytime, and for part of the year the southern hemisphere is tipped towards the Sun. The tilt gives each hemisphere opposite seasons. When it's winter in the UK, it's summer in Australia!

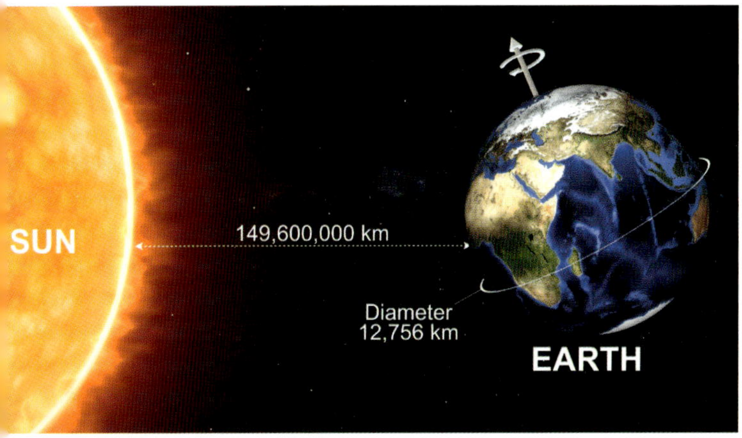

Holding it together

English scientist Isaac Newton explained in 1687 that gravity holds planets in orbit around the Sun. Gravity holds the Moon in orbit around Earth, and keeps you on Earth's surface. Getting to grips with gravity is vital for space travel.

Settling down

Earth started off so hot it was molten (liquid rock). The heavier materials sank, making a central core of metal. That's now wrapped in layers of rock, semi-molten deep inside but cool and hard on the surface, where we live. Much of the surface is flooded with water, and an atmosphere of gas covers everything.

FIND THE WAY

Which spacecraft has taken off from Earth? Follow the wiggly lines to find out.

Are you ready to leave Earth and set off to explore space? Let's go!

ANSWERS ON PAGE 68

GALAXY GLOSSARY

ORBIT Go around

BILLION One thousand million

ASTEROID Space rock

HEMISPHERE Half of a sphere

Early Earth

When Earth was newly formed, it was a very active place. There were no plants or animals yet, but the land was rocked by erupting volcanoes, earthquakes and asteroids smashing into the surface. Colour in this picture of early Earth.

FUN FACT
Asteroids delivered some chemicals vital to life.

MYSTERY PLANET

Some space scientists think there might be an undiscovered planet in our Solar System, orbiting beyond Neptune. What do you think it might look like? Draw it below.

First stop, the Moon

Earth has only one Moon – but it's a big one!

Making a Moon

Early in its life, Earth collided with another planet, called Theia. It crashed into Earth, blasting itself apart. Huge parts of Earth were also hurled into space. This first became a cloud of molten rock and gas, which then cooled into a ring of rock fragments. Over time, these stuck together making the Moon.

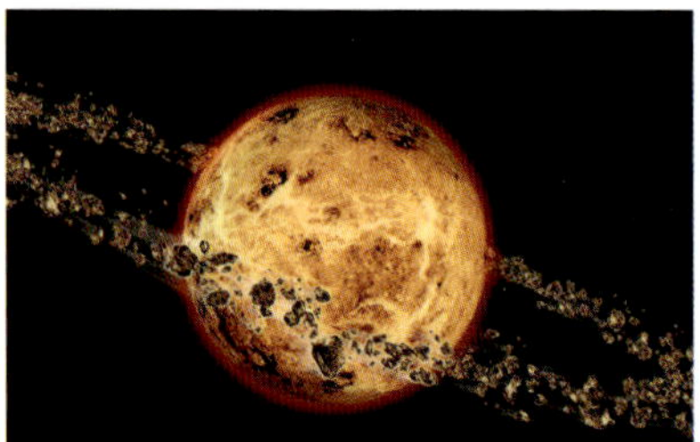

Sneaking away

The Moon formed much closer to Earth than it is now, at just 22,500 km away. It's now 17 times as far away! It would have looked much larger in the sky long ago. It's still creeping away at about 4 cm a year.

Shape shifting

The Moon takes 27 days to go around Earth. Its shape seems to change from a full circle to a thin crescent and back, depending on its position. When it's between Earth and the Sun, we see a dark new moon as sunlight falls only on the side of the Moon we can't see.

Is there a dark side?

We always see the same side of the Moon. The other side, which astronomers call the "far side", always faces away from Earth. This is because the Moon is tidally locked to Earth: it takes as long to turn on its axis once as to go around Earth.

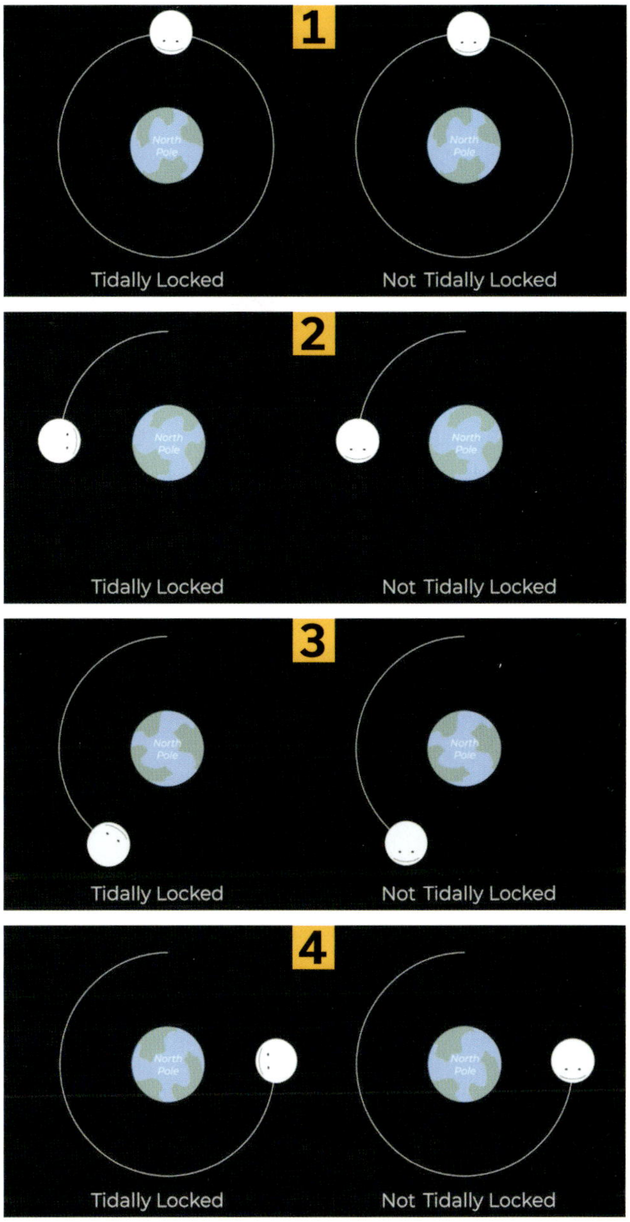

Illustration of tidal locking.

GALAXY GLOSSARY

ASTRONOMER Scientist who studies space

AXIS Line around which a turning object rotates

CRATER Hole in the ground made by an impact

ERODE Gradually wear away

Pits and pockmarks

The Moon is covered in craters made by asteroids smashing into the surface over billions of years. There is no weather on the Moon to erode the rock, and the surface isn't changed by volcanoes and earthquakes, so all the craters are still visible.

Safety first: wear a spacesuit!

Astronauts wear spacesuits when they go outside their spacecraft. What would happen if you went into space without a spacesuit? Find out with this fun activity.

PREPARE FOR SPACE!

You will need:

A GLASS BOTTLE

SMALL MARSHMALLOWS

A DRINK VACUUM PUMP AND ITS RUBBER STOPPER

Make sure you have all these materials

STEP 1

Drop several of the marshmallows into the bottle.

Pump it

STEP 2

Push the rubber stopper into the bottle. Use the pump to remove the air from the bottle.

Look

STEP 3

Look at the marshmallows! You wouldn't want that to happen to your body!

STEP 4

Take the stopper out of the bottle and watch the marshmallows to see what happens.

THINK ABOUT IT!

★ Imagine you are an astronaut, what would you take with you into space to remind you of home?

★ Imagine wearing a bulky spacesuit and trying to repair your spacecraft! Can you try tying your shoelaces while wearing a pair of thick gloves?

ASTRONAUT'S LOG

Date Completed

....

Was experiment a success?

....

Score out of 5? ....

Take a trip

To travel to the Moon you need a spaceship, but first you need to get it into space.

Let's go!

Spacecraft are launched into space with rockets. Burning lots of fuel blasts the craft upwards, escaping Earth's gravity by going really fast – at least 28,600 km/hour. Most rockets have stages, each with its own fuel. Once the fuel is used, the stage breaks away and falls back to Earth. Once it's high enough above Earth, the rocket releases the craft into space.

To the Moon ...

Outside Earth's atmosphere, in space, there is no air drag to slow down the craft. It no longer needs a streamlined, pointy shape and it only needs a little push from an engine to set it off in the right direction.

A rock and a hard place

On the Moon, there's no air or liquid water and the surface is made of rock and dust. Gravity is much weaker than it is on Earth, so astronauts feel light on their feet and can easily bounce and leap around! Their footprints will last thousands of years.

Moon rock

Apollo astronauts brought back rocks from the Moon between 1969 and 1972, and the Chinese craft Chang'e-6 returned rock from the far side of the Moon in 2024. From Moon rock samples, scientists can learn what the early Solar System was made of and how the Moon was formed.

... and back

To return to Earth, a spacecraft needs fuel to escape the Moon's gravity. But unlike take-off from Earth the craft doesn't need a lot of fuel, as there's no atmosphere to push through. Returning craft are kept light, with as little fuel as possible for take-off.

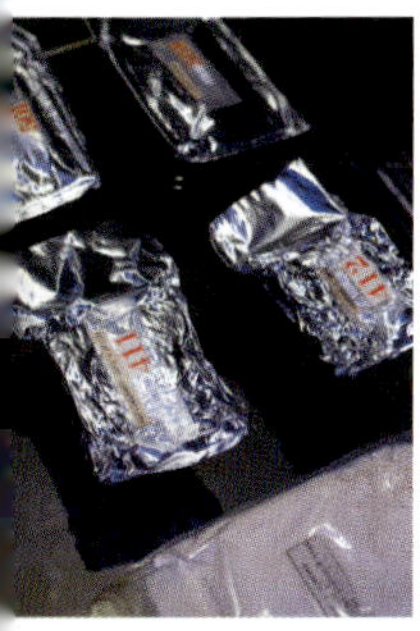

Take it and leave it

Astronauts must take everything they need, including food, water and even air. Because their craft needs to be lightweight to take off from the Moon, they leave nearly everything behind, from rubbish to Moon buggies and even a feather used in an experiment!

ROCKET READY?

Complete the picture using the grid as a guide to draw the other half of the rocket.

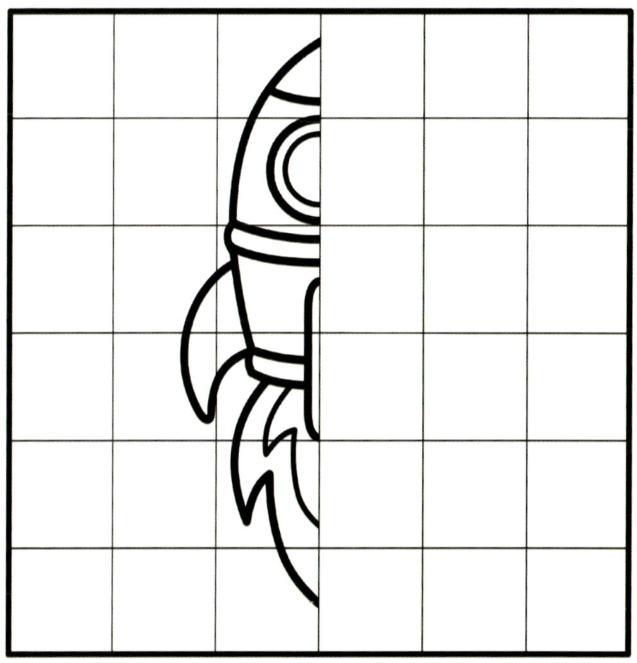

GALAXY GLOSSARY

GRAVITY: Force that pulls large objects towards other large objects such as Earth, other planets, the Moon, or the Sun.

MOON BUGGY: Lightweight vehicle used for transport on the Moon.

What a mess!

Astronauts leave behind almost everything that they take to the Moon, so there's a lot of junk lying around up there – probably 3,000 items! Can you find six matching pairs among the mess?

FUN FACT

Guess what? All the things shown in this picture really are on the Moon! Along with lots of bags of astronaut poo, dirty wet wipes and other nasty bits and pieces.

ANSWERS ON PAGE 68

Into space: meet the astronauts

Most astronauts don't go very far in space. They travel to work in a space station and stay inside it for weeks or months.

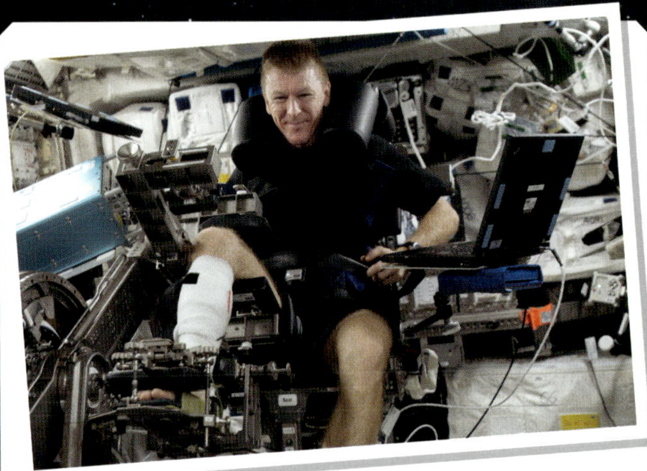

British Astronaut Tim Peake exercising in the ISS

Life in space

Being weightless causes problems with eyes, bones and muscles. Astronauts keep fit with daily exercises and have scans to check their bodies are healthy. Regular routines and frequent contact with their families help maintain their mental health. Food, medicines and other supplies are delivered, but water and air are recycled.

Name:
Yuri Gagarin
From:
USSR
Achievement:
First person in space, 1961
Spacecraft:
Vostok 1

Name:
Valentina Tereshkova
From:
USSR
Achievement:
First woman in space, 1963
Spacecraft:
Vostok 6

Name:
Alexei Leonov
From:
USSR
Achievement:
First person to walk in space, outside a spacecraft, 1965
Spacecraft:
Voskhod 2

Name:
Neil Armstrong
From:
USA
Achievement:
First person to walk on the Moon, 1969
Spacecraft:
Eagle (Apollo 11 Lunar Module)

Crew of the ISS, July 2024

On the ISS

The International Space Station (ISS) is a satellite. It's a huge space station built in space. Astronauts from many nations visit to carry out experiments and other work in space. Inside, they wear normal clothes and there is air to breathe. But they are weightless, so they and all their stuff floats around. It makes life tricky!

What's in a name?

The term for a person who has travelled in space differs depending on the Space Agency they were trained by. **Astronaut** is the more general term for **all space travellers** but originally meant those trained by the **United States**. A **cosmonaut** is trained by **Russia** and a **taikonaut** is trained by **China**.

GALAXY GLOSSARY

SATELLITE Object in orbit around a planet

SPACE STATION Spacecraft in permanent orbit above Earth with living and working space

UNTETHERED Without being connected to a safety line

Name:
Sally Ride
From:
USA
Achievement:
First American woman in space, 1983
Spacecraft:
Space Shuttle Challenger

Name:
Guion Bluford
From:
USA
Achievement:
First Black American astronaut in space, 1983
Spacecraft:
Space Shuttle Challenger

Name:
Bruce McCandless II
From:
USA
Achievement:
First untethered spacewalk, 1984
Spacecraft:
Space Shuttle Challenger

Name:
Helen Sharman
From:
UK
Achievement:
First British astronaut in space, 1991
Spacecraft:
Soyuz TM-11 and TM-12, Mir space station

Meet the neighbours: Rocks around Earth

Earth is one of four rocky planets in our Solar System. The others are very different from our planet!

Not all rocks are alike

The rocky planets all have a hard, rocky surface, that's about all they have in common. While Earth has a pleasant temperature, a breathable atmosphere and oceans of water, the others are inhospitable and dry, either very hot or very cold.

Mercury

Mercury is scorching by day at 430 °C (800 °F) and freezing at night, reaching -180 °C (-290 °F). It has a rocky outside and a metal core and possibly a layer of diamond 16 km (10 mi) thick in between! A day on Mercury is the same as 176 Earth days as it turns so slowly on its axis.

Venus

Venus has a dense atmosphere, it's hot, acidic and has immensely high pressure. Venus has a runaway greenhouse problem, with a layer of carbon dioxide clouds trapping heat so that the planet's surface is hot enough to melt lead. Venus is thought to have been more like Earth until 700 million years ago.

GALAXY GLOSSARY

ATMOSPHERE Layer of gas that surrounds a planet, also called air

METEOROID Small lump of rock in space

Mars

Mars is cold, barren and dusty. Winds whisk the dust into massive storms that can take months to settle. The atmosphere is so thin, heat escapes quickly. If you stood on Mars, your feet might be at a toasty 24 °C (75 °F) but your head would be freezing cold as heat hugs the surface!

How wrong can you be?

People had ideas about what these planets might be like long before we had spacecraft. In 1894, American astronomer Percival Lowell theorised that there were canals on Mars, perhaps made by Martians to move water around their planet. In the mid-20th century, people thought Venus might be a lush tropical world.

BRIGHT PLANET

Use the number guide to colour in the picture and find a rocky planet.

COLOUR BY NUMBER 1 2 3 4

Solar System race!

It's a race around the Solar System in the Space Olympics! Can you get your craft home first?

HOW TO PLAY THE GAME

1 You will need a dice and a counter, coin or very small toy for each player's spacecraft.

2 Place each spacecraft at the start.

3 Take turns to throw the dice and follow the route. The blue arrows move you forwards, the red arrows move you back. If you land on a yellow ringed planet, you miss a go.

4 The winner is the first to get home to Earth!

Let's explore Mars

Of all the planets in the Solar System, Mars is most like Earth.

Hunting for Martians

People have long been fascinated by Mars and wondered whether anything lives there. Exploration of Mars has revealed a cold, dead world with fierce dust storms that could not support life as we know it. Scientists now look for evidence of life long ago.

Eyes all around

The craft sent to Mars have been orbiters (which stay in space), landers (which land on the surface) and rovers (which land and move around). They all send data and photos back to Earth using radio waves. Orbiters can scan the whole surface from above, while landers and rovers study a small area.

Exploring Mars:

1964: Mariner 4: Launched '64. First photos of another planet's surface from space taken in '65.

1975: Viking 1 and 2: photographed the entire surface, showing lava plains, volcanoes and canyons.

1996: Sojourner (first Mars rover): investigated conditions for planning future missions.

2003: Spirit and Opportunity (rovers): investigated geology to see how the Mars landscape formed.

Collecting evidence

Robotic rovers explore the planet's surface by sampling rocks and testing the atmosphere. Rocks collected by the Perseverance rover have been stored on Mars and could one day be returned to Earth. Some rocks have chemical traces suggesting microbes lived there long ago.

A wetter past?

Mars has ice at its poles and vast underground reservoirs of water. Its atmosphere is too thin for water to stay on the surface as liquid now, but Mars would have had flowing water on the surface once, making conditions good for life.

GALAXY GLOSSARY

MICROBE Living thing too small to see without a microscope

GEOLOGY The chemical make-up of rocks and the study of rock

LAVA Liquid molten rock from within a planet

ROBOTIC TWINS

Can you find and circle 10 differences between these two Mars rovers?

ANSWERS ON PAGE 68

2005: Mars Reconnaissance Orbiter: looked for areas with a watery past worth exploring with landers.

2011: Curiosity (rover): investigated the chemistry of Mars, looking for signs indicating earlier life.

2020: Perseverance (rover) and Ingenuity (helicopter): looked for evidence of ancient microbes and stored rock samples for later collection.

Make a Mars helicopter

The Ingenuity helicopter that accompanied Perseverance had to fly in the very thin atmosphere of Mars. You can make a helicopter that can fly on Earth, but you won't have the chance to try it out on Mars!

WHIRL INTO SPACE!

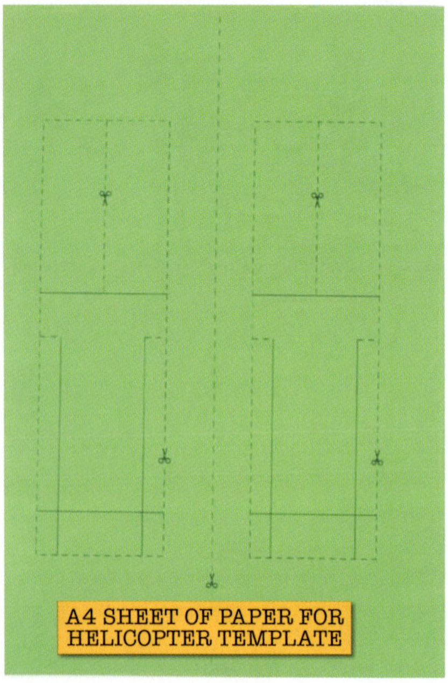

A4 SHEET OF PAPER FOR HELICOPTER TEMPLATE

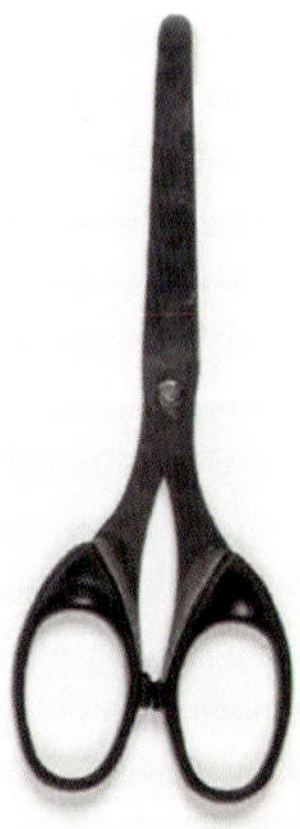

SCISSORS

PAPERCLIP

TOP

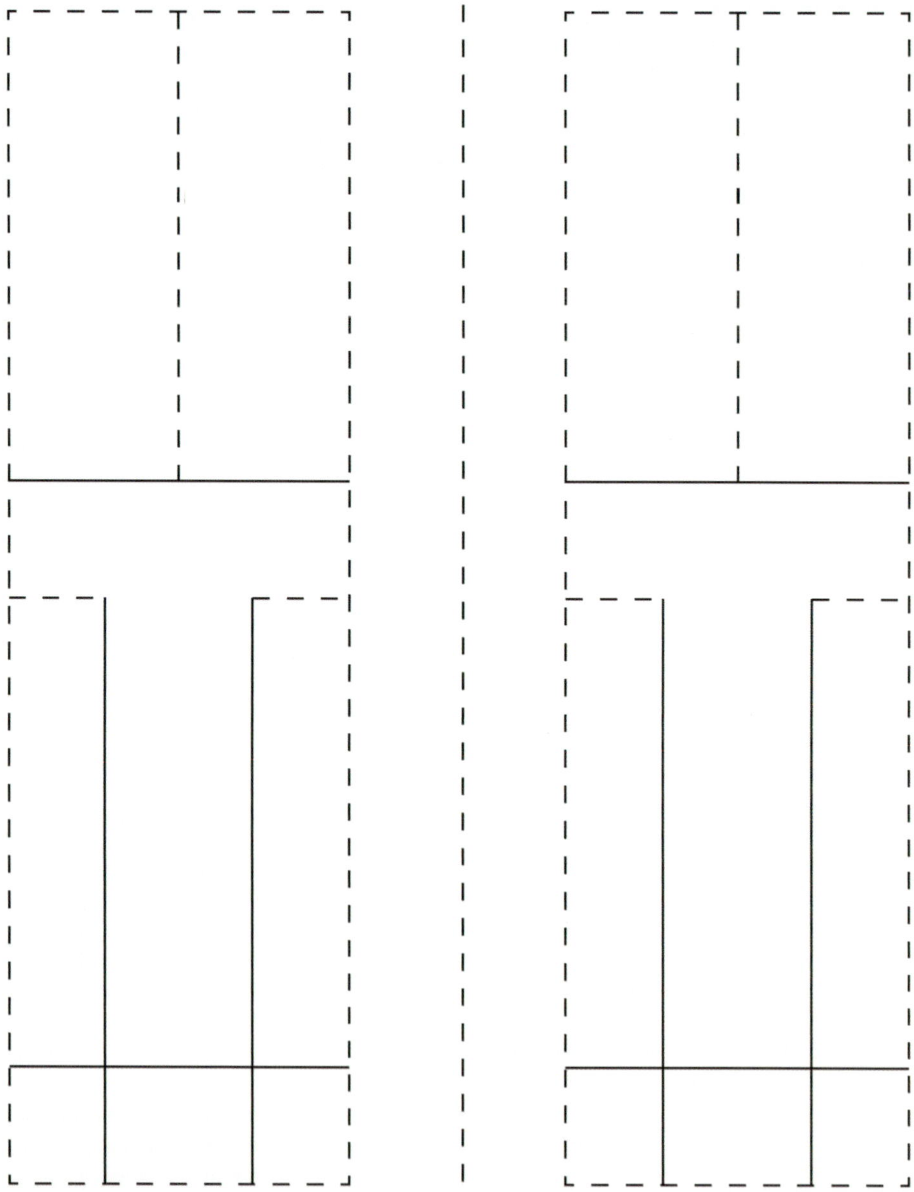

BOTTOM

Make sure you have all these materials.

STEP 1

Trace the helicopter template onto your sheet of paper and then cut along the dotted lines.

ASTRONAUT'S LOG

Date Completed ....

Was experiment a success? ....

Score out of 5? ....

THINK ABOUT IT!

★ What would you take with you to pass the time on a three-year mission to Mars?

★ A day on Mars is 40 minutes longer than an Earth day. Do you think you'd notice the extra minutes in your day? What would you do with the extra time?

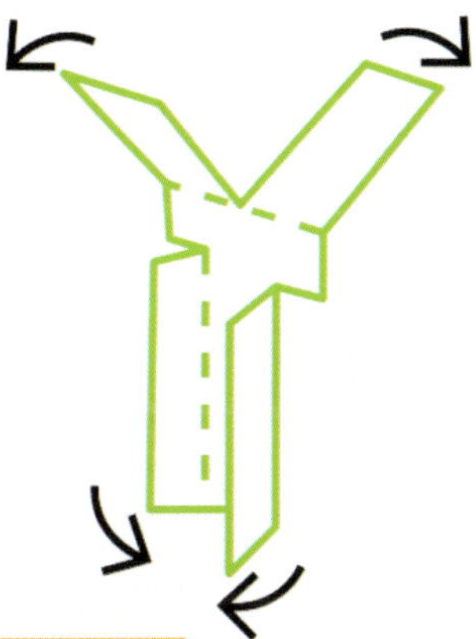

STEP 2

Fold along the solid lines

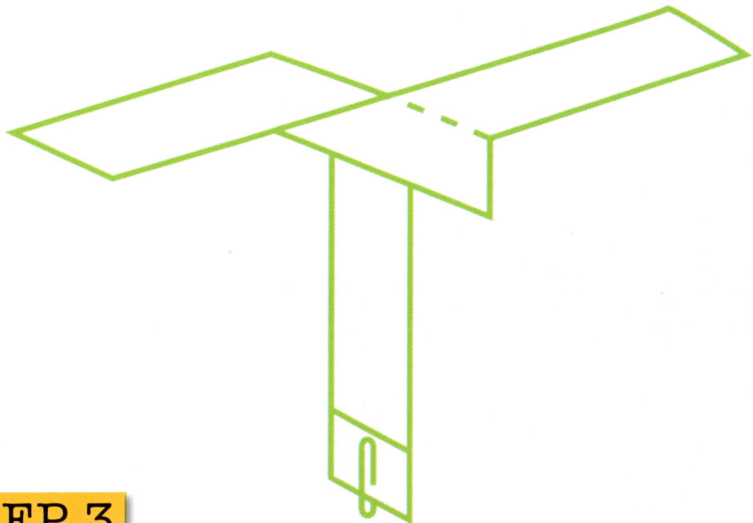

STEP 3

Put the paper clip over the bottom of the helicopter to hold the sides together and give it weight.

STEP 4

Hold your helicopter as high as you can, then let it go. It should spin to the ground.

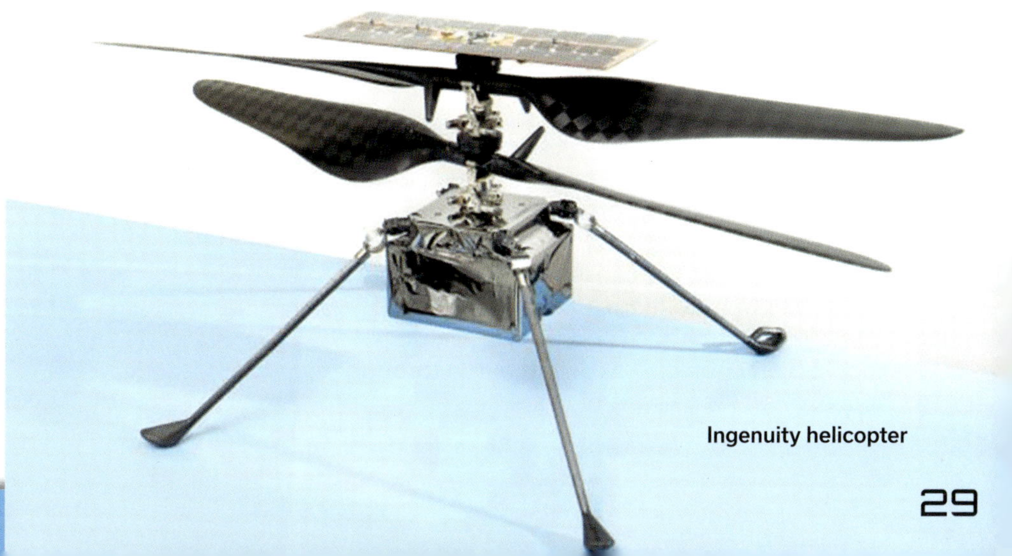

Ingenuity helicopter

Visitors from space

Not everything in space stays there. Some space rocks fall to Earth.

Lumps and leftovers

When the planets formed, leftover dust, ice and gas gathered into large rocky objects (much smaller than planets). These orbit the Sun as asteroids. We can learn about the early Solar System from them. Collisions between asteroids, planets and moons have also knocked off chunks of rock that hurtle through space, often for millions of years.

Catastrophe!

Very rarely, a huge asteroid smashes into a planet. Around 66 million years ago, an asteroid 10 km across slammed into Earth. It caused catastrophic fires, tsunamis, earthquakes and climate change. More than half the living things on Earth died, including all the non-bird dinosaurs.

From meteoroid to meteor to meteorite

When a small rock breaks off from an asteroid it is called a meteoroid. If it enters Earth's atmosphere, it usually burns up, appearing as the fiery streak of a meteor (often called a shooting star). If it survives to reach the ground, then it's called a meteorite.

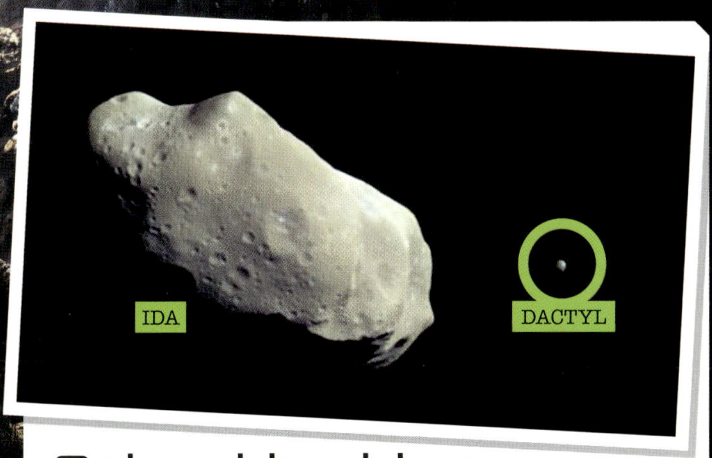

Asteroids at home

The Asteroid Belt is an area between Mars and Jupiter that contains billions of asteroids. Some are solid rocks, while others are loose collections of rubble. Asteroids are widely spaced, so you wouldn't be able to see from one to the next. A few are nearly big enough to be planets. Some, like Ida, have their own mini-moons!

GALAXY GLOSSARY

TSUNAMI Giant wave that floods on to land

Ice and rock

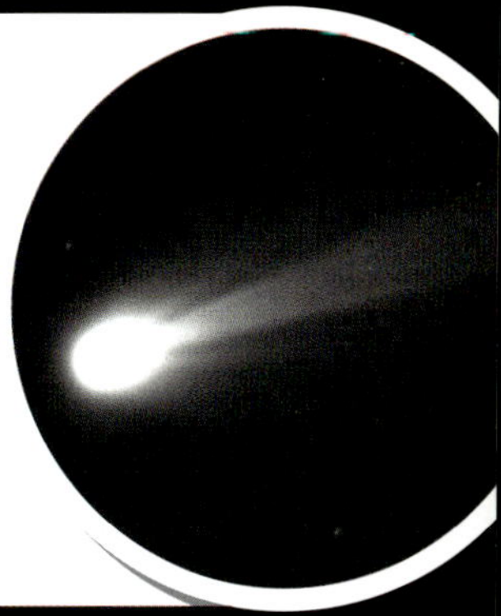

Comets have an icy heart: they're lumps of ice mixed with rock dust that orbit the Sun. As they approach the Sun, some ice melts giving the comet a tail of dust and gas that glows in the sunlight. Some we see every few years, but some take thousands of years to return.

A visitor from far away

In 2017, astronomers spotted the first object to have come from outside the Solar System. Named *'Oumuamua*, it was a long, narrow lump of rock or ice that tumbled through space. It went past the Sun and back into interstellar space.

CODED MESSAGE!

Reveal a secret message by drawing in the missing lines on each picture so they each match the image here. The first one has been done for you.

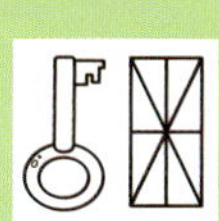

ANSWERS ON PAGE 68

Asteroid oddities

Asteroids aren't shaped like planets, they're more irregular in size and shape and they can look very different depending on which angle you're looking at. Can you match up the big asteroid pictures with the named smaller pictures?

1 Psyche (223km)

2 Mathilde (53km)

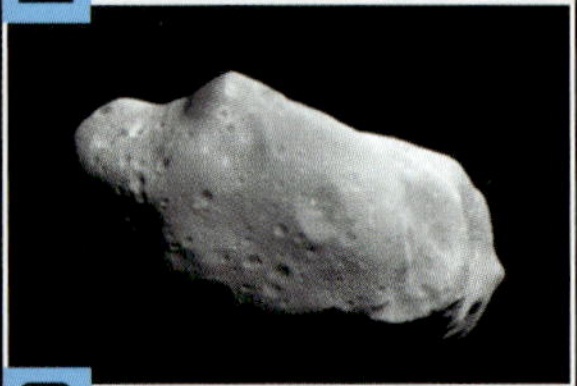

3 Ida (60 km)

4 Lutetia (120 km)

5 Vesta (525km)

6 Eros (34 km)

7 Ceres (962km)

MATCH THE ASTEROIDS

A ....

B ....

FUN FACT
Spacecraft have landed on asteroids, and even taken samples of them.

D

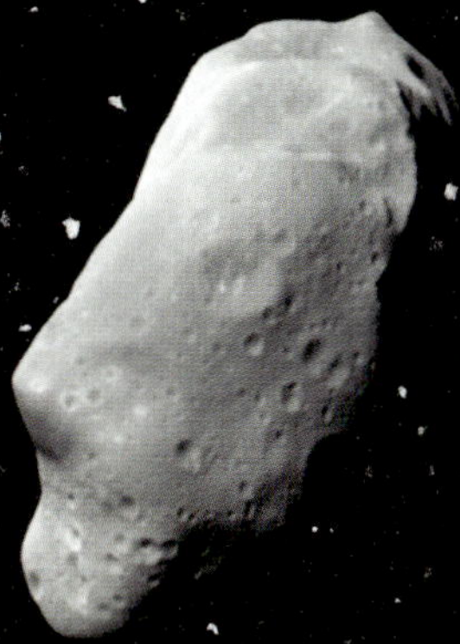

E

C

G

F

ANSWERS ON PAGE 68

Meet the neighbours: The weird ones

While the planets near the Sun are rocky, those beyond the Asteroid Belt are made of gas and ice.

Giants in space

Gas planets Jupiter and Saturn are huge – about ten times the width of Earth. Like the Sun, they are made mostly of the light gases hydrogen and helium. They have no solid surface, but scientists think they might have a small rocky core.

Making a ball of gas

As the Solar System formed, the heavier dust and rock moved towards the Sun, but the lighter gases drifted further out. They clumped together, growing into vast icy clouds. The gravity of their huge mass pulled the gas towards the middle, putting it under great pressure and making round planets.

Hot or cold?

The gas and ice planets get denser towards their centres. Their gas becomes like soup or slushy ice as the particles are pushed so close together they can't move around. But it's hot ice, as the temperature increases with the pressure!

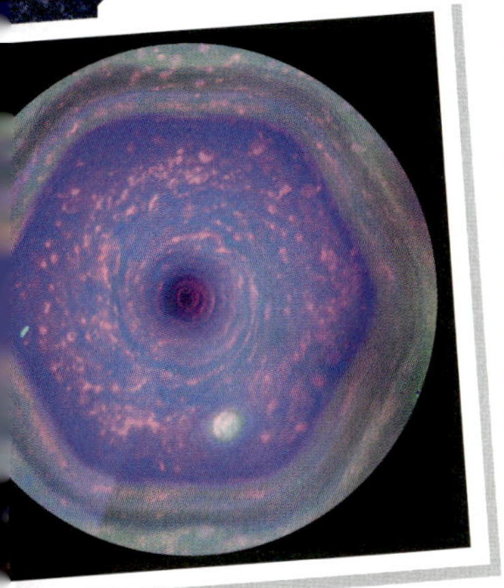

Bad weather

Jupiter is striped with bands of cold clouds whipped around by strong winds. Its Red Spot is a storm that has raged for hundreds of years. Saturn has a six-sided jet stream at its North pole known as 'the hexagon', centred on a wild hurricane 50 times the size of any on Earth.

Hard rain

The ice giants Neptune and Uranus are mostly made of water, ammonia and methane which were probably frozen ice grains when the planet formed. Like the gas giants, they are denser and hotter towards the middle – up to 6,727 °C, so hot and dense that carbon escapes from the methane and falls as diamond rain!

GALAXY GLOSSARY

METHANE Gas made of carbon and hydrogen, it is best known as natural gas, used as a fuel

AMMONIA Gas made of nitrogen and hydrogen, it's used to make fertiliser and cleaning products

JET STREAM Narrow, fast-moving stream of air or gas, also known as wind

Rings and moons

Gas and ice giants have many moons, some very small and some quite bizarre shapes and structures. They also have rings of rock and dust whirling around them. Oddly, Uranus's rings go top to bottom because the planet tipped over at some time.

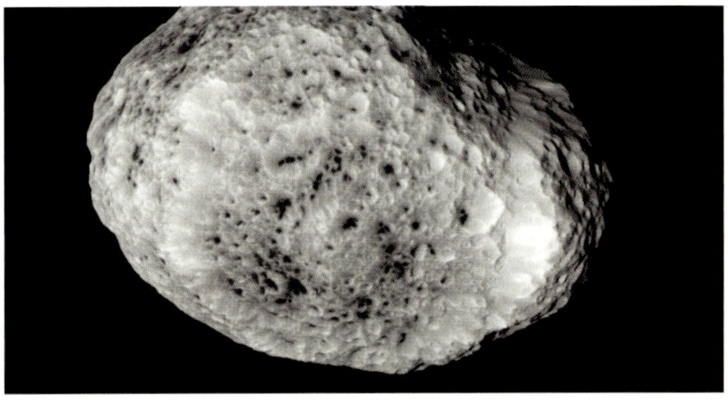

Pan (Saturn)

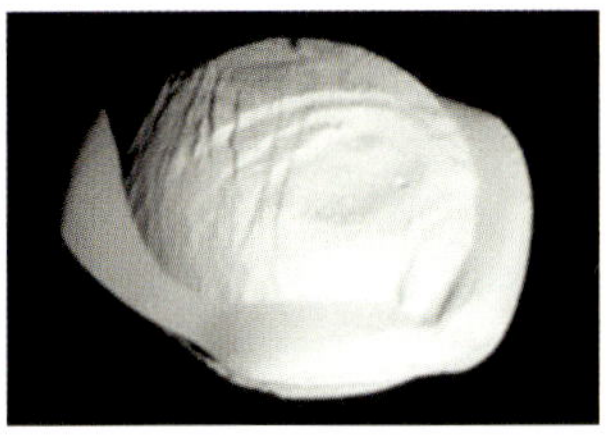

Pan (Saturn)

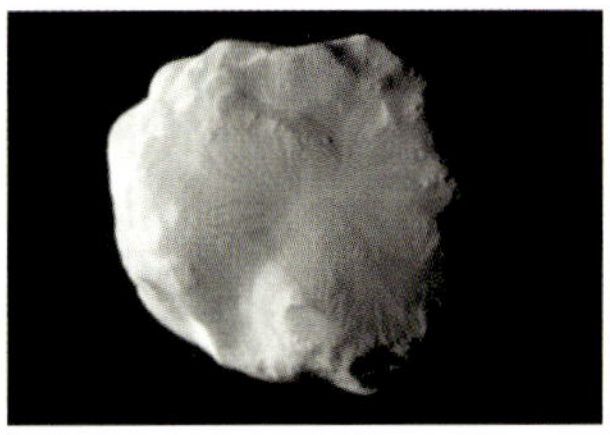

Helene (Jupiter)

SOLAR SYSTEM TOUR

Can you plot a route through space that visits all three planets? Start at the black arrow.

ANSWERS ON PAGE 68

Make an edible comet

Comets are made mostly of ice, stuck together with some dust in a blobby shape. Follow these instructions to make your own edible comet! If you want a rockier comet, stir some sprinkles or chocolate drops into the milky mixture.

ALLERGY NOTE: THIS RECIPE CAN ALSO BE MADE WITH NON-DAIRY MILK

You will need:

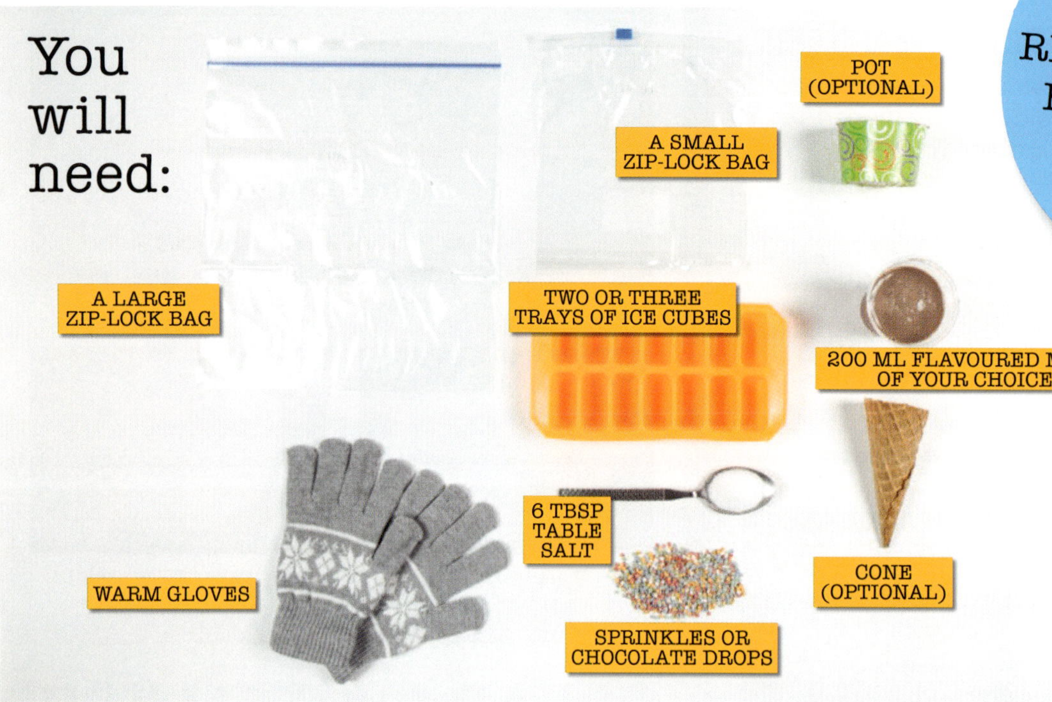

Make sure you have all these things before you start.

STEP 1

Pour the flavoured milk into the **small** zip-lock bag. (If you're using them add the chocolate drops or sprinkles at this stage.) Seal the bag shut.

STEP 2

Tip the ice and the salt into the **large** zip-lock bag. The salt will lower the melting point of the ice, so you might see the ice start to melt.

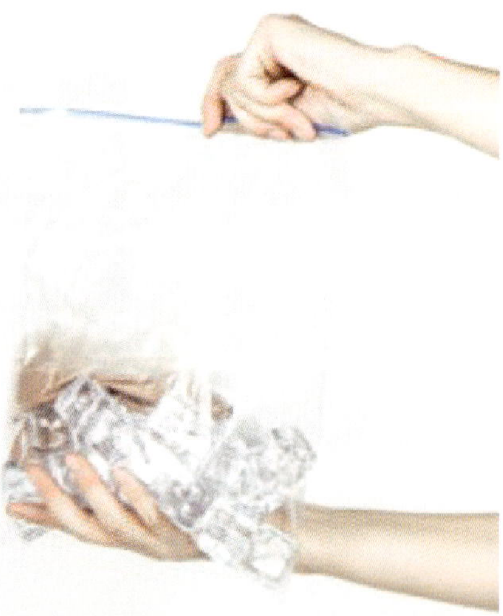

STEP 3

Check the **small** bag is still securely sealed, then place it inside the **large** bag of salty ice. Then seal the **large** bag shut.

THINK ABOUT IT

★ Did you know that astronauts can eat real ice cream when they're up in space? What other treats would you bring with you?

★ Astronauts have to bring all their food with them on missions. What food do you think would be tricky to eat in space?

ASTRONAUT'S LOG

Date Completed ....

Was experiment a success? ....

Score out of 5? ....

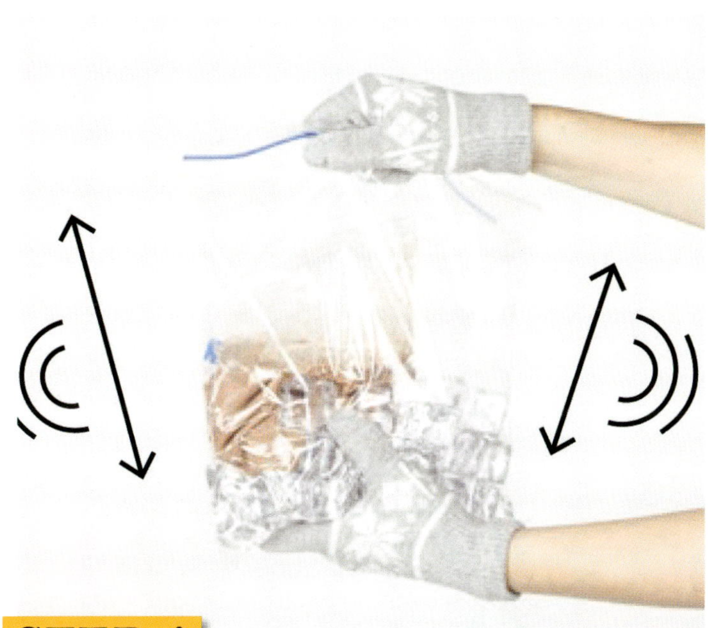

STEP 4

Put on the gloves (so that your hands don't get too cold) and gently shake and squeeze the two bags. Try to surround the small bag with the salty ice mix. Do this for about five minutes or until the mixture looks frozen.

STEP 5

Open the large bag, remove the small bag and wipe off any salty water from the outside of the bag. Carefully tip your frozen comet core into a bowl or cone. Add more sprinkles or chocolate drops and enjoy your space snack!

Robots in space

Astronauts have been to space and to the Moon, but uncrewed craft have explored much further.

Up, down, round and round

The first spacecraft to make it to space was the satellite Sputnik, launched by the USSR (a large country that included modern-day Russia), in 1957. It orbited Earth sending radio bleeps for three weeks and burned up in Earth's atmosphere after three months. It was not robotic, as it couldn't accept instructions, but it began the Space Age and the Space Race.

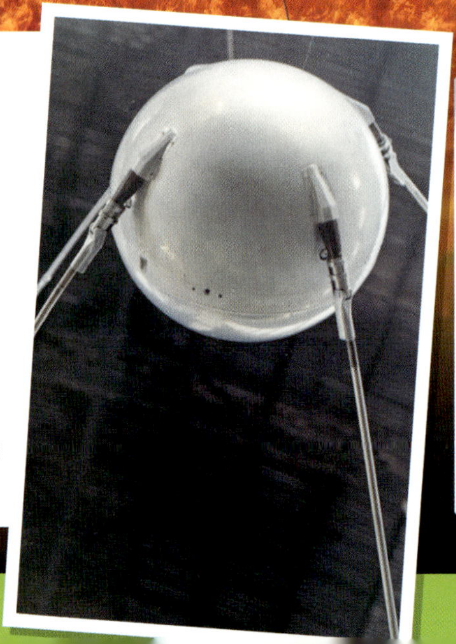

Going places

Since then, spacecraft have made 'flyby' missions to all the planets in our Solar System, sending back photos and data. Many probes have settled into orbits to study a planet for months or years. Some have set down landers for a closer look. Others have visited asteroids, comets, moons of other planets, or even flown close to the Sun.

Why robots?

Robotic craft don't need food, water or air. They don't get lonely, sick or bored. They can go to places that are dangerously hot or cold and take years to reach. And yet they can do nearly everything human astronauts can do.

Up close

A probe can show us far more than we can discover with telescopes. It can take astonishing photos, map the whole surface of an object in space and investigate its composition. Some can even collect samples and return them to Earth for further study.

Storms on Jupiter, photographed by Juno, 2018

Keep in touch!

Probes keep in touch using radio signals. They are partly controlled by instructions sent from Earth, and their programming also lets them work independently. A message takes up to 20 minutes to reach Mars, but over four hours to reach Neptune or Pluto, so working independently is important.

GALAXY GLOSSARY

PROBE Uncrewed spacecraft that goes beyond Earth's orbit

ROBOTIC Controlled remotely by radio, or by its own programming

SPACE RACE The race between the USA and the USSR, from 1960 to 1980, to make progress in space exploration

Spacecraft Timeline

1962: Mariner 2, first flyby of another planet, Venus

1965: Mariner 4, flyby of Mars

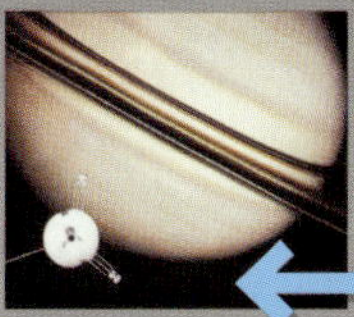

1973: Pioneer 10, flyby of Jupiter

1974: Mariner 10, flyby of Mercury

1979: Pioneer 11, flyby of Saturn

1986: Voyager 2, flyby of Uranus, then of Neptune in 1989

2001: NEAR Shoemaker, landed on the asteroid Eros

2004: Stardust, collected material from comet Wild 2, returning it to Earth in 2006

2005: Cassini, dropped the Huygens lander on Saturn's moon Titan

2005: Hayabusa, returned material from asteroid 25143 Itokawa

2014: Philae landed on the comet 67P/Churyumov-Gerasimenko

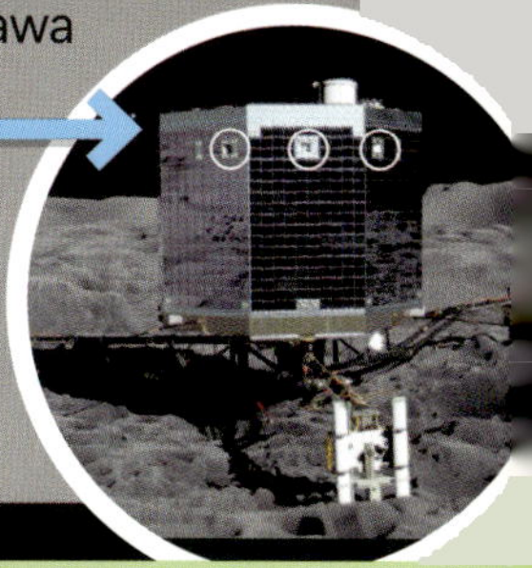

2015: New Horizons, flyby of Pluto

2024: Chang'e 6 returned dust from the far side of the Moon

PROBING AROUND

Can you fill in the missing probe in each line? Every row and column must have only one of each type.

ANSWERS ON PAGE 68

Crowded space

Many probes have flown around the Solar System. Some have been deliberately crashed into planets, but a lot are still going. Can you count up all the different spacecraft in this crowded patch of space?

ASTRONAUT'S CROSSWORD

Use the picture clues below to help complete this space crossword.

ANSWERS ON PAGE 68

Into the stars

The Sun is our own star at the centre of our Solar System. It's a fairly average star that is similar to many others.

How stars work

Stars are giant balls of gas. They are so massive that their force of gravity puts the centre under immense pressure. The pressure forces atoms of hydrogen to combine in nuclear fusion, making another light gas, helium. The energy released becomes the light, heat and other radiation of sunlight — or starlight.

Star makers

Stars form when huge clouds of gas and dust collapse under the force of gravity. They grow in areas of galaxies called 'star nurseries'. Our galaxy is the Milky Way, which is still making new stars all the time.

Westerlund 2 star nursery in Milky Way

Life and death in space

Over billions of years, a star will burn through all of its fuel (hydrogen gas). Really big stars generate enough heat to burn other fuels (carbon and helium). But, ultimately, once all its fuel is gone a star will start to cool down. What happens next depends on the star's size ...

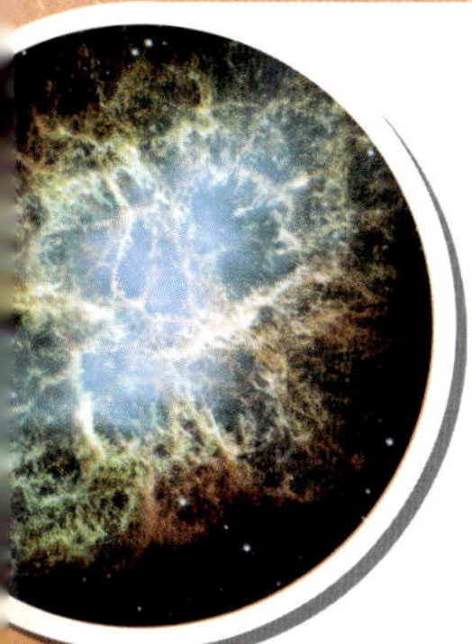

Life after death?

Our Sun will eventually swell into a glowing red giant. Its outer layers will drift outwards as a 'planetary nebula' of gas and dust around a tiny white dwarf star. A larger star collapses into itself and then blasts apart in an explosion called a supernova, leaving a black hole or a neutron star.

Putting out the recycling

Further chemical elements are made in the explosion of a supernova. All the matter from the star is hurled out into space. It becomes part of the clouds of gas and dust where stars are made and can eventually be recycled into new stars and planets.

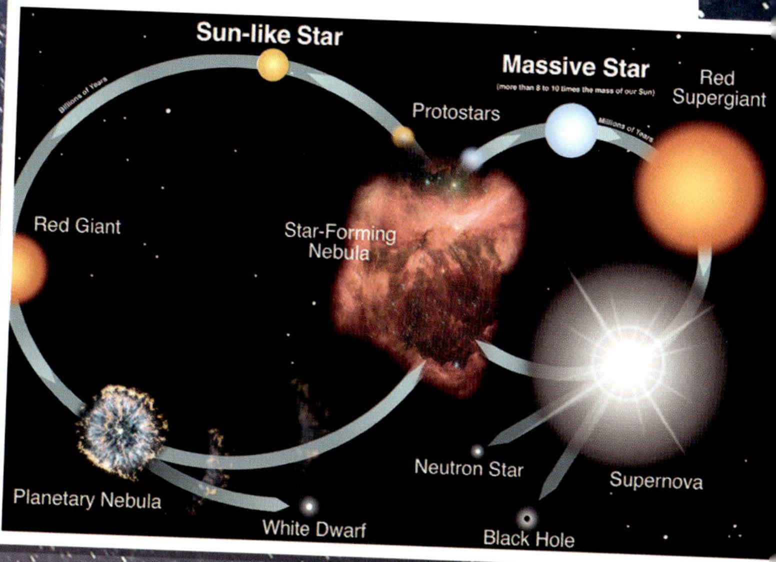

GALAXY GLOSSARY

ATOMS The basic building block of matter

NUCLEAR FUSION Process of forcing atoms to combine (fuse) to make a single larger atom

ELEMENT One of the basic 118 chemicals that make up all matter in the universe

GALAXY A huge area containing hundreds of billions of stars

PLANETARY NEBULA Cloud of dust and gas around a dying star

OFF TO EXPLORE!

Can you guide the astronaut to her rocket so she can explore the universe?

ANSWERS ON PAGE 68

Make the Milky Way

Galaxies are often a swirling mass of stars. Our Milky Way is a spiral galaxy like this. You can make your own image of a swirling galaxy using milk!

WARNING, THIS IS NOT SOMETHING TO DRINK, SOAPY MILK WILL NOT TASTE NICE!

You will need:

Make sure you have everything you need before you start.

STEP 1

Put the tray on a flat surface and pour a little milk into it, just covering the bottom.

STEP 2

Add a few drops of food colouring to the milk, dotted around near the centre of the tray.

STEP 3

Pour a little washing-up liquid into a cup and dip a cotton bud in it.

STEP 4

Now dip the cotton wool bud gently into the milk and watch the colours swirl!

THINK ABOUT IT

★ If you wanted to give your milky galaxy stars, you could sprinkle in some biodegradable glitter before you add in the washing-up liquid.

★ This isn't how galaxies are made, of course, but forces including gravity often give them swirling spiral shapes. Where else do you see spiral shapes in nature here on Earth?

ASTRONAUT'S LOG

Date Completed

....

Was experiment a success?

....

Score out of 5? ....

Exploring outer space

The Solar System is our local neighbourhood, but it's only a very tiny part of space. There's a whole big universe out there!

A long way to go

It took the New Horizons probe nine years to reach Pluto. Going beyond the Solar System would take an incredibly long time. Even at the fastest a spacecraft has ever travelled, it would take over 6,000 years to reach the next nearest star, Proxima Centauri.

Light-years away

Astronomers measure distances in space in light-years, which is amount of distance that light travels in a year. As light travels at 300,000 km per second, it's a long way! Proxima Centauri is just over four light-years away. That's about 40 trillion km.

Very Large Array radio telescope

Galileo Galilei

Using an early telescope in 1609, the Italian scientist Galileo discovered that the planets are other worlds, some with their own moons, and that the Milky Way is a band of stars.

Telescopes in space

Powerful telescopes in space, like the Hubble Space Telescope and the James Webb Telescope, reveal details of nearby planets and of distant galaxies, some of them millions of light-years away. When we see something this distant, we are seeing it in the past, when the light left it. It might no longer be there!

GALAXY GLOSSARY

INTERSTELLAR Between stars

ULTRAVIOLET Electromagnetic radiation with a wavelength a bit shorter than that of visible light

Reaching out

Four probes launched in the 1970s are now flying through interstellar space. Voyagers 1 and 2 will drift near other stars in about 40,000 years, and Voyager 2 will approach Sirius, the brightest star in the sky, in 296,000 years. Pioneer 10 will swing by another star in 90,000 years.

Peering into the void

We can't travel to other stars, but we can look at them with telescopes. Telescopes can detect light or other types of electromagnetic waves, such as radio and ultraviolet. We can use them to see very distant objects, and to find out about their temperature and composition.

SPACE MATCH

Check out this ringed planet. Can you identify and circle its matching shadow?

ANSWERS ON PAGE 68

Patterns in the stars

For thousands of years, people have seen pictures in the patterns that stars make in the sky. Can you find these constellations in the patch of starry sky? There is one yellow star in each constellation. Draw lines to join the stars when you find them.

NOT ALL STARS SHOWN WILL BE USED

FUN FACT

The patterns people see in the stars don't relate to any real link between those stars. The stars are all very, very far away from each other.

CAN YOU FIND THESE CONSTELLATIONS IN THE STARRY SKY?

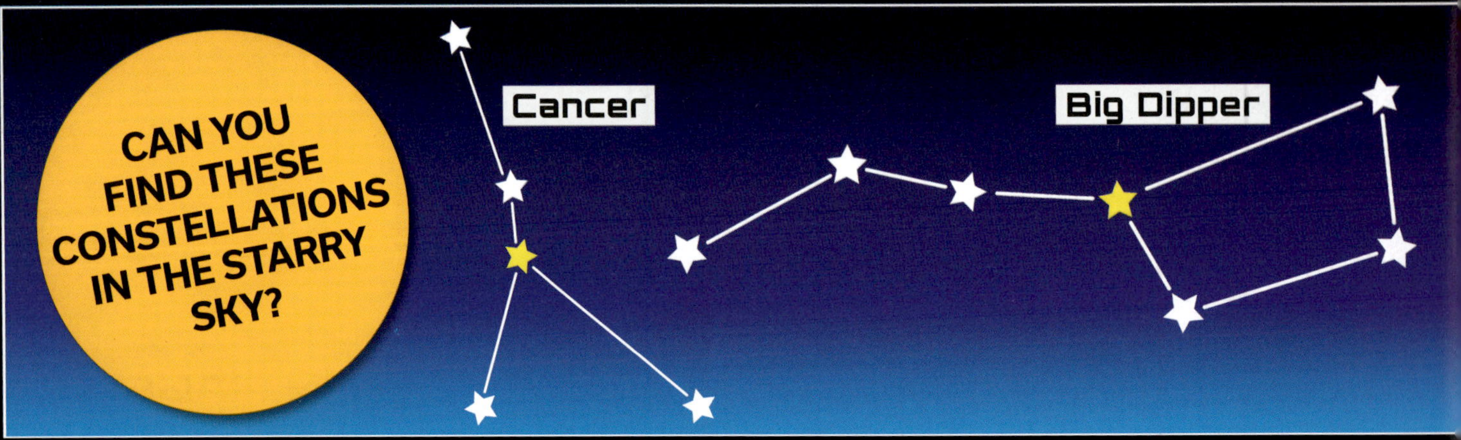

CREATE A CONSTELLATION

Invent a constellation of your own. How many stars will represent your picture? What will you name it?

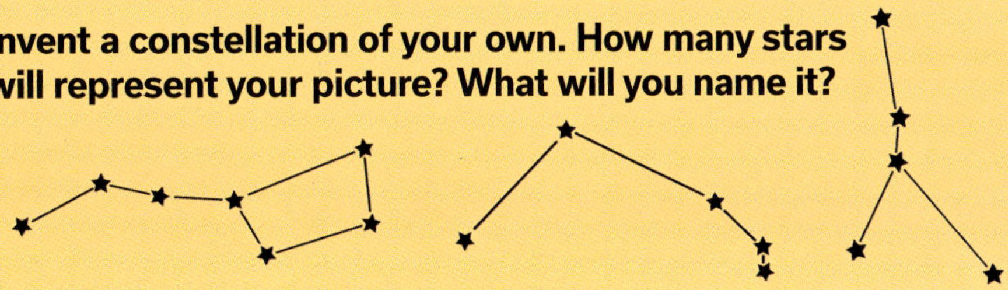

Constellation name: ....

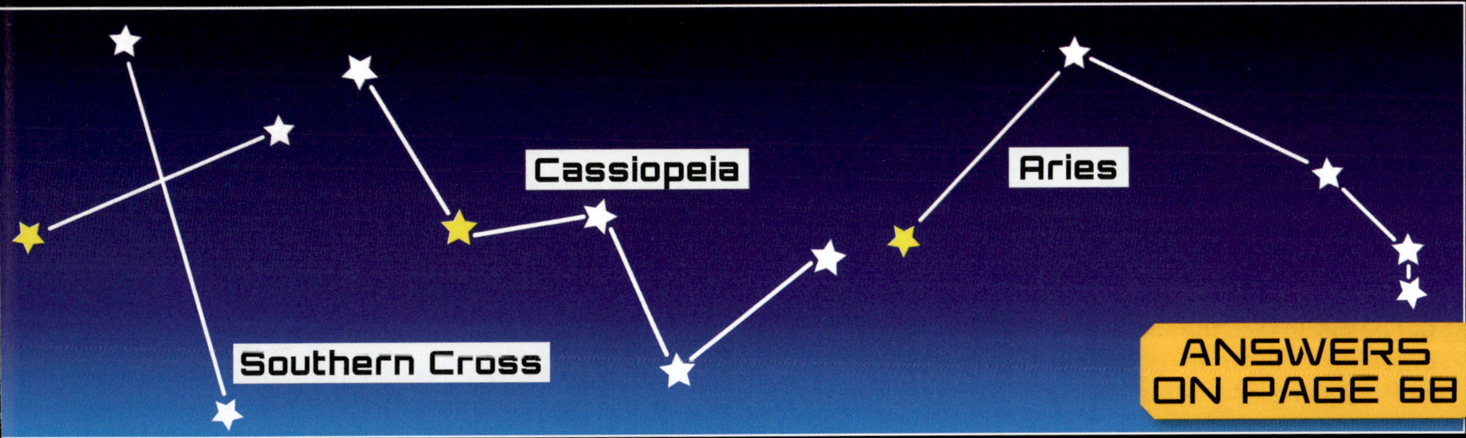

ANSWERS ON PAGE 68

The universe beyond

The universe extends far beyond the Solar System and even beyond our galaxy, the Milky Way.

Stars in 3D

When we look at the night sky, we see the stars as though they are spread over a curved surface above our heads. In fact, they are not on a surface but at different depths from us. The constellations would not look the same if seen from anywhere else in space.

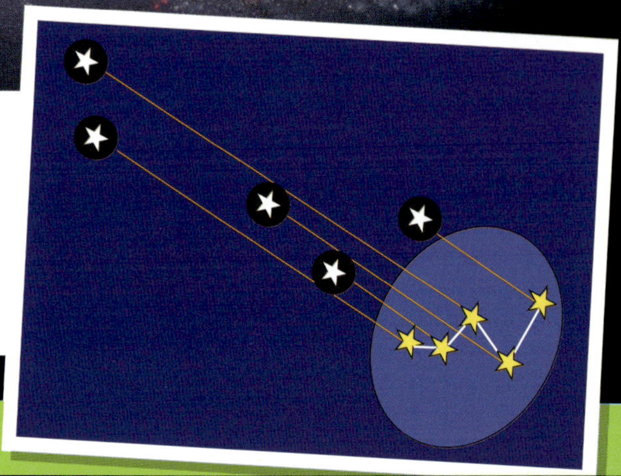

The vast universe

Astronomers talk of the 'visible universe', which is how far we can see with our most powerful telescopes and is a sphere centred on Earth, 93 billion light-years across (41.5 light-years in every direction). The entire universe might be much, much bigger, we just can't see that far (yet)!

The view from here

If you go somewhere very dark, with no light pollution, you can easily see the Milky Way. It looks like a bright band across the sky. As we are inside the Milky Way, we are looking across its disc and don't see it as a spiral.

Our home in space

All the stars we can see in the night sky are from within our own galaxy, the Milky Way. It's a spiral galaxy with a bright, dense centre, and then curved 'arms' swirling out into space with more bands of stars. Our Solar System is on one of the arms.

GALAXY GLOSSARY

LIGHT POLLUTION Light from towns and traffic that gives the sky a dull glow so it is never truly dark

Galaxies abound

Galaxies are vast collections of stars. The Milky Way holds 100-400 billion stars, and there are hundreds of billions of galaxies in the universe! Galaxies are grouped in clusters. The nearest galaxy to ours, the Andromeda galaxy, is nearly 2.5 million light-years away.

Deep Field. In 1995, over a period of ten days, the Hubble Space Telescope photographed a black patch of sky near the Big Dipper. The result was incredible. We were able to look back in space and time to observe around 3,000 different galaxies.

HOW MANY?

How many aliens can you find in the picture?

ANSWERS ON PAGE 68

Keep away from the edge!

There is a black hole in the middle of every galaxy, left behind by large stars. Here matter is so dense, and gravity so strong, that not even light can escape, so black holes look like gaps in space. Anything too close will get dragged in. Can you steer the spaceship back from the edge of this black hole to safety? Avoid bumping into anything else too!

HIDDEN WORDS

Can you find all the space words in this puzzle? When you have finished, colour in the pictures.

PLANET

Y	W	P	Z	X	H	D	G	U	F	O
X	J	G	S	T	A	R	J	Z	W	Y
A	Y	P	T	A	G	U	A	E	T	A
S	D	H	W	P	T	E	W	S	U	N
T	C	A	E	L	D	Y	J	D	G	Z
R	W	U	Y	A	C	U	E	H	N	R
O	D	Y	A	N	E	H	D	U	Y	O
N	J	A	G	E	G	A	E	W	T	C
A	P	H	J	T	L	R	G	X	J	K
U	N	T	E	L	E	S	C	O	P	E
T	H	G	T	W	J	Y	Z	H	D	T

TELESCOPE

ROCKET

ASTRONAUT

SUN

STAR

UFO

ANSWERS ON PAGE 68

Before, now, after

The universe is vast now, but astronomers believe it started off really, really, really tiny!

Beginning with a bang

Most astronomers think the universe began with a tiny point, smaller than an atom, nearly 14 billion years ago. This suddenly expanded in an event they call the Big Bang (though there was no noisy 'bang'). Everything that would become the matter and energy in all of the universe started here.

Still growing

The new universe expanded in an instant. In a hundredth of a billionth of a trillionth of a trillionth of a second it doubled in size 90 times, becoming the size of a grapefruit or small ball. It's still expanding, but more slowly now. As it spread out, it cooled from unimaginably hot to how it is now – quite cold.

EVOLUTION OF THE UNIVERSE

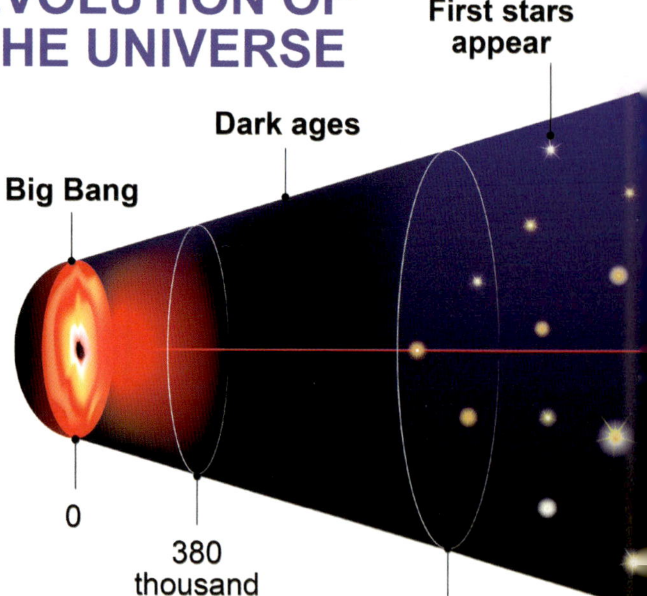

GALAXY GRID

Can you complete the grid? Make sure each space item appears only once in every row and column.

ANSWERS ON PAGE 68

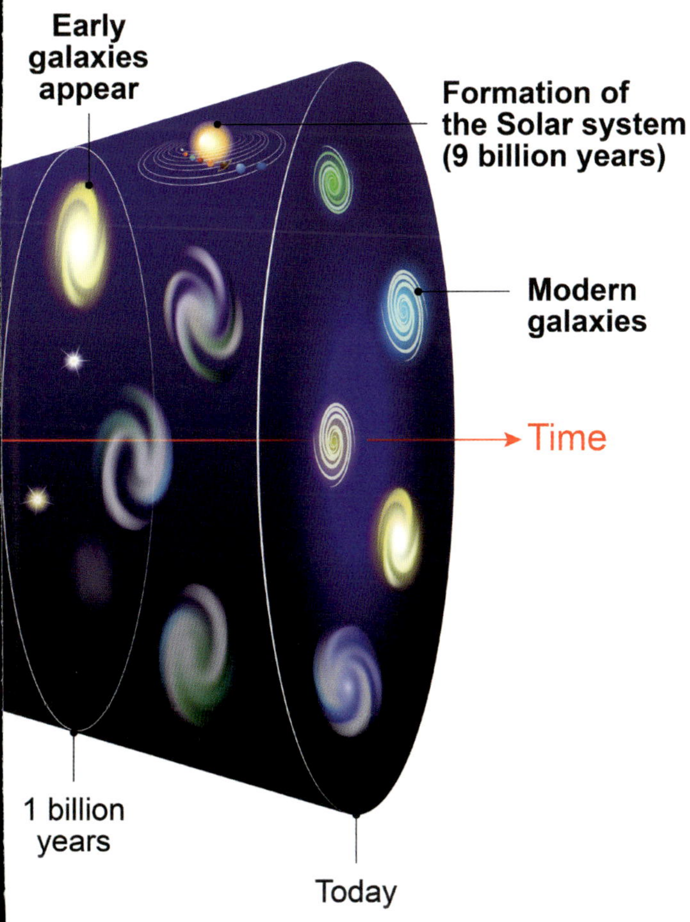

GALAXY GLOSSARY

MICROWAVES Electromagnetic radiation with wavelength shorter than radio but longer than visible light

Orange universe!

A flash of light soon after the Big Bang lit up the universe with orange light. Over billions of years, the wavelength of that energy has stretched. They are now microwaves, which we can pick up with special telescopes.

What's the matter?

Hydrogen and helium gases were the first matter to form. Within a few hundred million years, clouds of gas collapsed to make the first, huge stars. Through nuclear fusion, they made other types of matter.

Hello, sunshine

The first stars were so hot they glowed blue-white. They were very short lived, and probably ended in massive supernovas after just a few million years. The matter they made reformed into later stars and then planets. Our sun emerged less than five billion years ago.

What next?

We don't know whether the universe will keep expanding until everything is really far apart from each other and become cold, lifeless and still. It might instead stop expanding and collapse and explode all over again. Or it might continue to grow steadily and keep adding matter so it gets bigger and bigger. Whichever it is, it will happen billions of years from now.

Expand the universe!

The expanding universe doesn't expand into anything as there is nothing outside it. Instead, things in it just move further apart as space appears between them. You can see how it works by making your own expanding balloon-iverse!

You will need:

BLOW UP THE UNIVERSE!

PERMANENT MARKER

STICKERS

BALLOON

CLIP

RULER

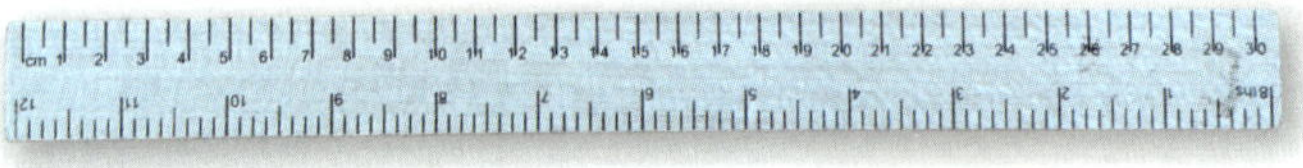

Make sure that you have all the things you need.

STEP 1

Partly inflate the balloon. Use the clip to close the end tightly so that the air doesn't escape.

STEP 2

Stick stickers on the balloon and draw a wiggly line along the balloon with the marker pen. This represents a wave of light. Use your ruler to measure the length of the line and the gaps between some of the stickers and make a note of these.

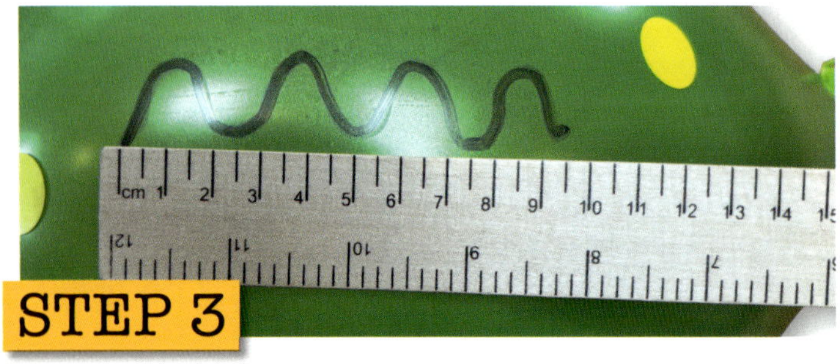

STEP 3

Unclip the clip and fully inflate the balloon, before clipping it again. Now measure the gaps between spots and the length of the wave of light.

What do you discover?

ASTRONAUT'S LOG

Date Completed

Was experiment a success?

Score out of 5?

THINK ABOUT IT

★ Have the stickers that represent stars or galaxies changed size? Has the distance between them changed? What does this tell you about the real universe expanding?

★ Your wiggly line (wavelength) has got longer. How does this relate to the real universe?

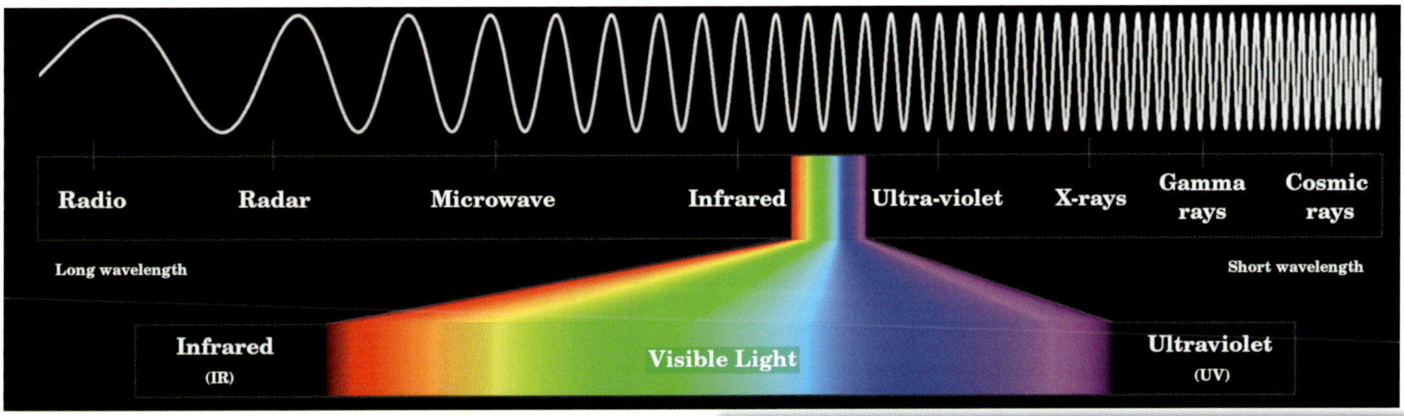

Are we alone?

Earth is the only place that we know for sure that life exists. But could life be found elsewhere in the universe?

Looking for life

One reason we explore space is to investigate whether life is rare or common – whether Earth is perhaps unique in having life or whether life starts easily and is found elsewhere. For most of Earth's history, only simple life forms existed. These are what we are most likely to find elsewhere.

Near neighbours

So far, it doesn't look likely there is advanced life in the Solar System beyond Earth. There might have been microbes on Mars in the past. Oceans beneath the surface of some of the moons of gas giants, like this one, might have some form of life – we don't know yet.

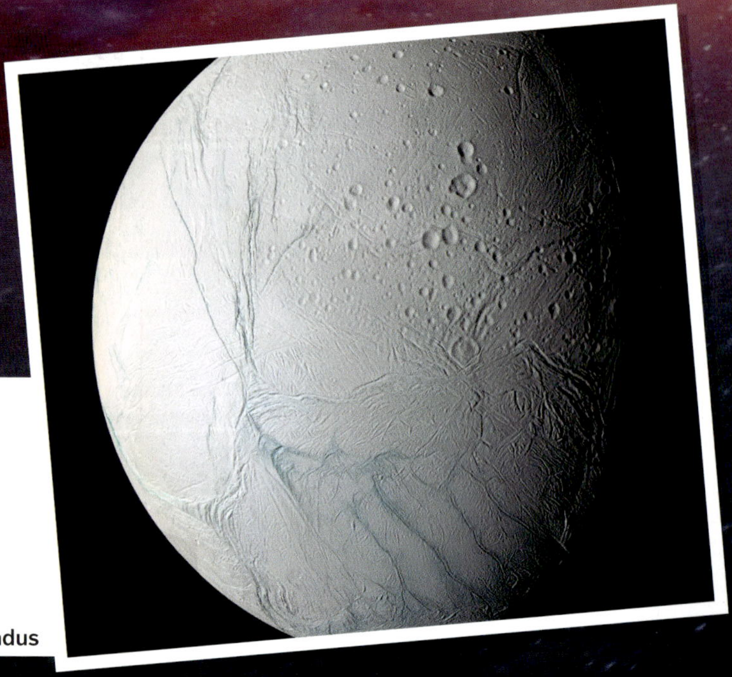

Saturn's moon – Enceladus

GALAXY GLOSSARY

EXOPLANET Planet orbiting a star other than our Sun

Looking for intelligence

We might be able to tell if a planet has conditions suitable for life, but not what type of life it has, if any. Intelligent beings with technology might send radio signals into space. Astronomers search for these but haven't found any yet. Microbes or non-technological civilisations would be hard to spot.

A message from us

We have sent a few radio messages into space, carefully constructed so that they can be understood without knowing human languages. Plaques on the Voyager and Pioneer craft give some information for any alien life that find them. And the Voyager craft carried a Golden Record with sounds and images of Earth.

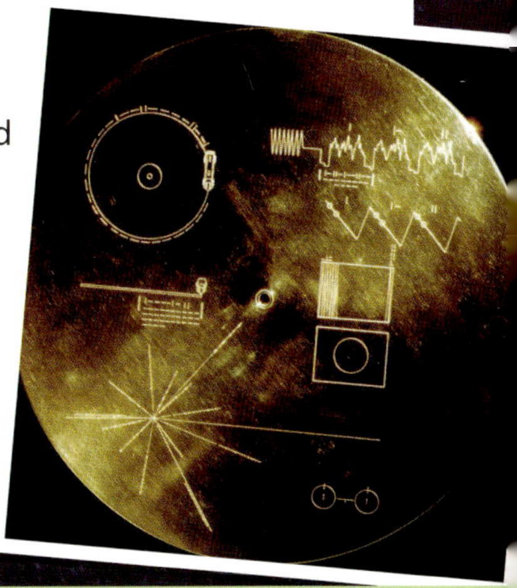

Far away

Most stars probably have at least one orbiting planet, so there are lots of places life could be hiding. Astronomers have found planets around other stars and by using radio telescopes and other instruments, they can investigate whether these exoplanets are made of rock or gas, their temperature, size and distance from their Sun.

WHERE FROM?

Can you work out which alien spacecraft belongs with which exoplanet?

ANSWERS ON PAGE 68

Hello, aliens!

Any intelligent aliens we find won't speak our language, and we won't speak theirs. We will need to use computers to try to understand any communications. See how good you might be at cracking an alien code!

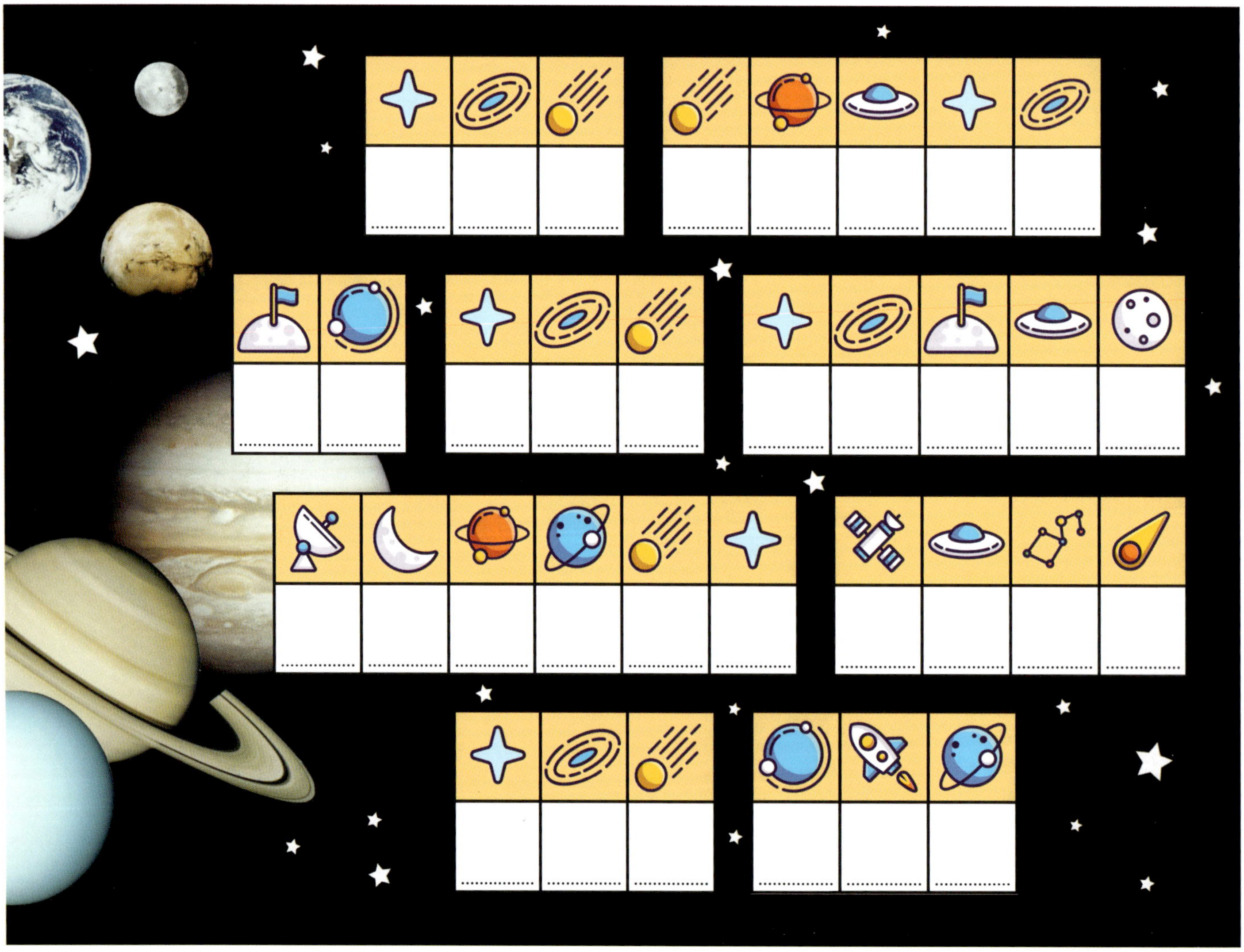

MATCHING PLANETS

The telescope has recorded the same exoplanet twice. Can you see which one it is?

ANSWERS ON PAGE 68

Where next?

So far, humans have only travelled to the Moon, and sent probes around and beyond our Solar System. What might we do next?

A place in space

A base, where humans can live on the Moon, is on the space wish list. This would make it easier to study the Moon and how it formed in more detail. A base would also be a staging post for expeditions further afield — to other planets, moons and asteroids.

GALAXY GLOSSARY

SOLAR WIND: Charged particles pouring from the Sun into space

Off to Mars?

A crewed mission to Mars would help us explore that planet. Technical issues, and the challenges of sending people so far away for so long, mean this won't happen very soon. But several groups are making plans. A colony on Mars would need to produce its own food and recycle water and air.

Probing moons

The search for life in the Solar System will take us to moons like Saturn's Enceladus where water shoots through ice volcanoes from an ocean of liquid water, which instantly freezes before being ejected into space. We could sample this water to look for evidence of microbes (an early form of life).

Off to the stars

The stars are too distant for us to send craft to visit them now. But new ideas for propelling spacecraft might one day give us faster travel. At a tenth the speed of light, a spacecraft could reach the next-nearest star system with planets in 43 years. Too long for a human crew, but not for a robotic craft!

Blown by sunlight?

One idea is to use sunlight or solar wind to propel a craft with a solar sail, rather like a sailing ship pushed by the wind. With nothing to slow it down in space, a spacecraft with a solar sail would go faster and faster as more sunlight or solar wind hit it.

TELL US APART

See if you can find 10 differences between this picture of two astronauts setting off for an adventure in space. When you have finished, colour them in.

ANSWERS ON PAGE 68

Build a Moon base

Many designs for a base on the Moon or Mars are low-lying domes. These use the least amount of materials for the area covered but are very strong. On Mars, a domed shape would also protect against violent dust storms. Can you design and make your own space base?

You will need:

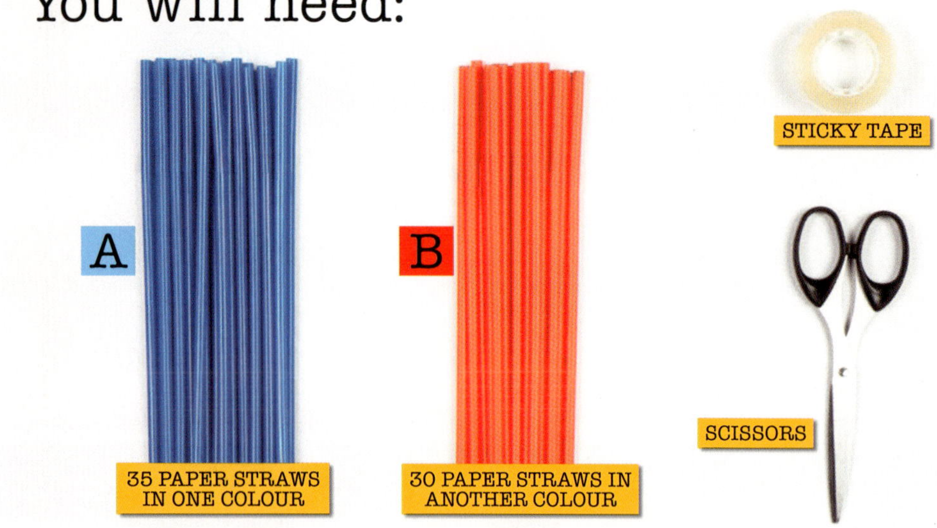

WOULD YOU WANT TO LIVE ON THE MOON?

Make sure you have everything you need before you start.

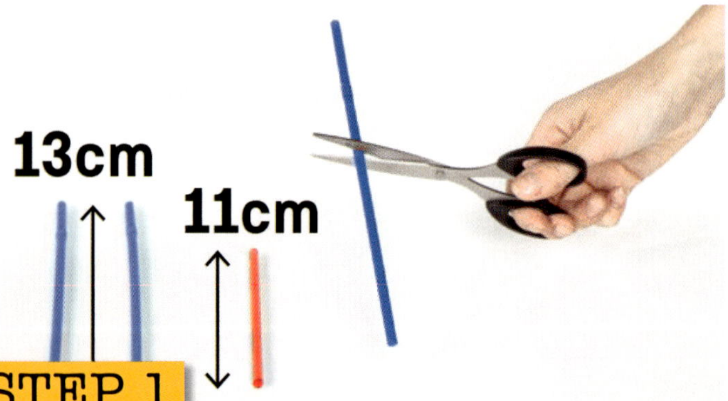

STEP 1

Cut the 35 straws (**A**) to 13 cm. Cut the 30 straws (**B**) to 11 cm.

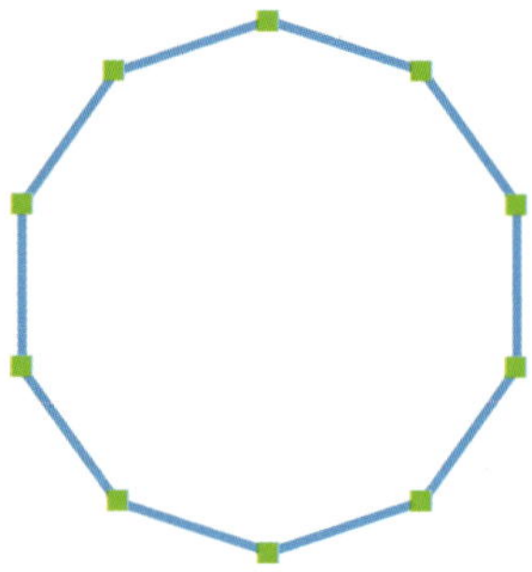

STEP 2

Begin building your dome by creating a base of 10 straw **A**s stuck together with tape, as shown..

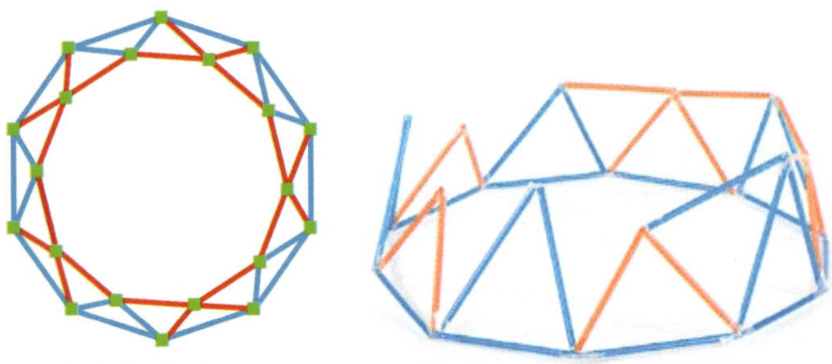

STEP 3

Tape 10 straw **A**s and 20 straw **B**s together in connected triangles as shown.

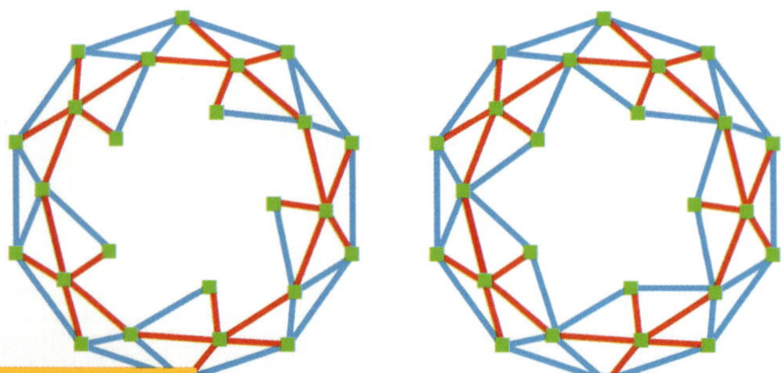

STEP 4

Continue sticking the straws together, following these diagrams.

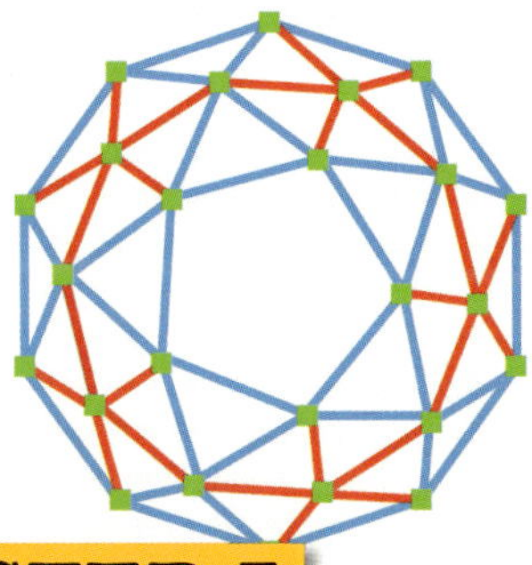

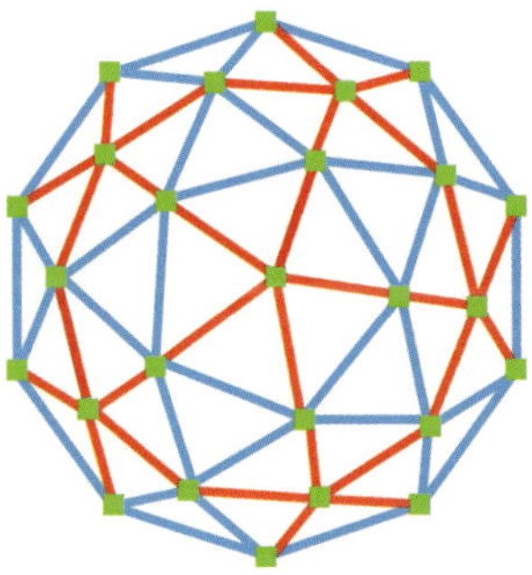

STEP 5

Finally, fill in the last straws to complete the dome.

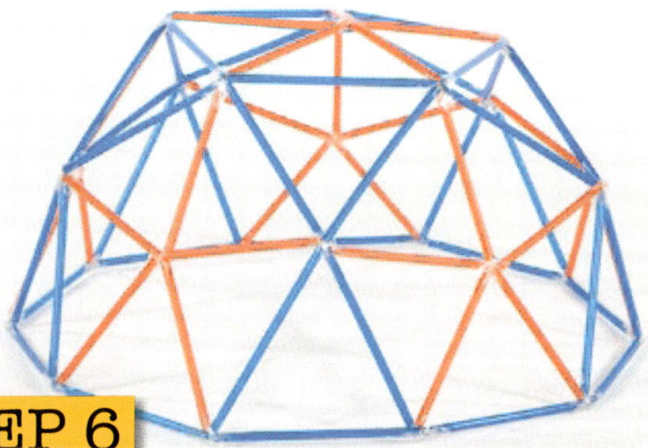

STEP 6

Your finished dome should look like this – just like the image shown above.

ASTRONAUT'S LOG

Date Completed

....

Was experiment a success?

....

Score out of 5? ....

THINK ABOUT IT

★ People living on the Moon would have to grow plants for food. Do you think they would grow them in the same dome they lived in?

★ What materials do you think would be good to build a dome on the Moon? What would you put in your space dome?

Could you be an Amazing Astronaut?

You've learned a lot about space and how we explore it. Do you think you have learned enough to become an astronaut? Try this Amazing Astronaut quiz and find out!

1 Which is the safest place to visit?

A. Venus ☐
B. The Moon ☐
C. Mercury ☐
D. The Sun ☐

2 If you needed diamonds to fix a special instrument in your spacecraft, where could you get them?

A. Venus ☐
B. Mars ☐
C. A comet ☐
D. Jupiter ☐

3 If you were visiting a colony on Mars where would it get its food from?

A. Meteor showers ☐
B. They would grow their own ☐
C. Sent from Earth ☐
D. Mars' rocks are edible ☐

4 Why can't you visit a nearby star system?

A. It takes too long to get there ☐
B. We don't know the way ☐
C. You can't escape the gravity of the Solar System ☐
D. No planets to land on ☐

5 You're revising for your space exam. Who was the first person to go into space?

A. Neil Armstrong ☐
B. Brian McCandless ☐
C. Yuri Gagarin ☐
D. Helen Sharman ☐

6 If you were in space and saw a star go supernova, what would you do?

A. Go towards it for a closer look ☐
B. Keep as far away as possible ☐
C. Put your protective space gear on ☐
D. Nothing – it's light-years away, so no need to worry ☐

7 A small rock has fallen to Earth from space. You want to log it in your records. What do you call it?

A. An asteroid ☐
B. A comet ☐
C. A meteor ☐
D. A meteorite ☐

8 You have been recruited to go on a space journey that will take two years to go and return, with a few months' research at your destination. Where are you most likely to be going?

A. A moon of Saturn ☐
B. Mars ☐
C. An exoplanet ☐
D. The Moon ☐

9 Imagine you were on a trip to Jupiter. You've been given lots of advice, but some of it is wrong. Which one of these statements should you ignore?

A. It's very windy ☐
B. It's very hot near the middle ☐
C. Look out for dust storms! ☐
D. It has no solid surface ☐

10 If you had to fly through the Asteroid Belt. Where would you be going?

A. Mars ☐
B. Neptune ☐
C. Mercury ☐
D. Phobos ☐

11 Which of these things would you NOT find on the Moon?

A. A Moon buggy ☐
B. Abandoned cameras ☐
C. A feather ☐
D. An old Apollo command module ☐

12 Which of these DON'T you need to worry about if you visit the International Space Station?

A. Your food will float away ☐
B. Your body might lose bone and muscle mass ☐
C. You will need to wear a spacesuit all the time ☐
D. It's really hard to wash your hair ☐

HOW DID YOU DO?

Check the answers to see how many questions you got right.

1–4 Good job, your astronaut training is going well.

5–8 Great score, your knowledge is blasting off!

9–12 Well done, your skills are out of this world!

ANSWERS ON PAGE 68

ANSWERS

PAGE 09
Spacecraft B has taken off from Earth

PAGE 32/33
1. G, 2. F, 3. E, 4. C, 5. D, 6. A, 7. B

PAGE 35

PAGE 47
Planet 2

PAGE 59

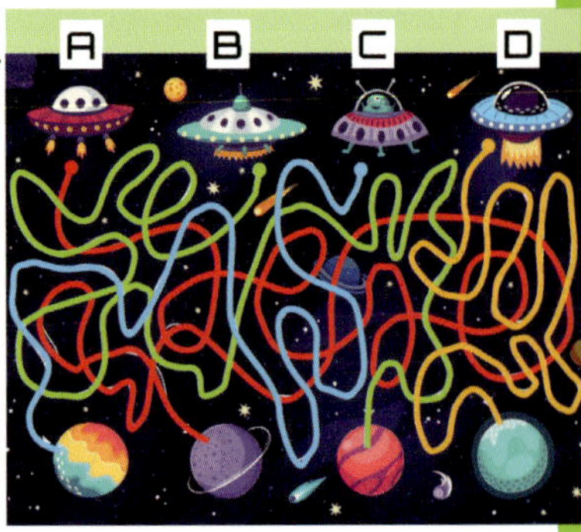

PAGE 48/49

PAGE 18/19
1. Flags
2. Golf balls
3. Moon boots
4. Cameras
5. Feathers
6. Tissues

PAGE 39
1. A, 2. B, 3. D, 4. C

PAGE 40
A. 9, B. 12, C. 10, D. 11, E. 15

PAGE 41

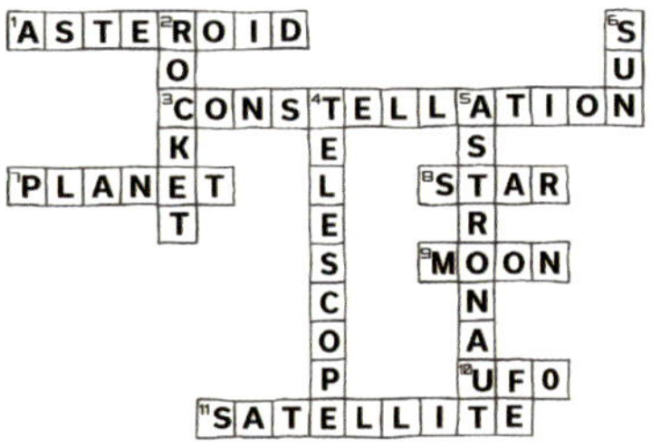

PAGE 51
There are 7 aliens

PAGE 52

PAGE 60
The Earth is the third planet from the Sun

PAGE 61
J and I are the same.

PAGE 27

PAGE 63

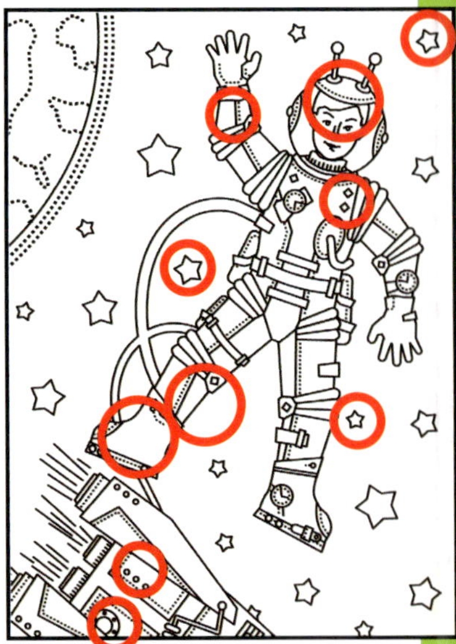

PAGE 43

PAGE 53

Y	W	P	Z	X	H	D	G	U	F	O
X	J	G	S	T	A	R	J	Z	W	Y
A	Y	P	T	A	G	U	A	E	T	A
S	D	H	W	P	T	E	W	S	U	N
T	C	A	E	L	D	Y	J	D	G	Z
R	W	U	Y	A	C	U	E	H	N	R
O	D	Y	A	N	E	H	D	U	Y	O
N	J	A	G	E	G	A	E	W	T	C
A	P	H	J	T	L	R	G	X	J	K
U	N	T	E	L	E	S	C	O	P	E
T	H	G	T	W	J	Y	Z	H	D	T

PAGE 31

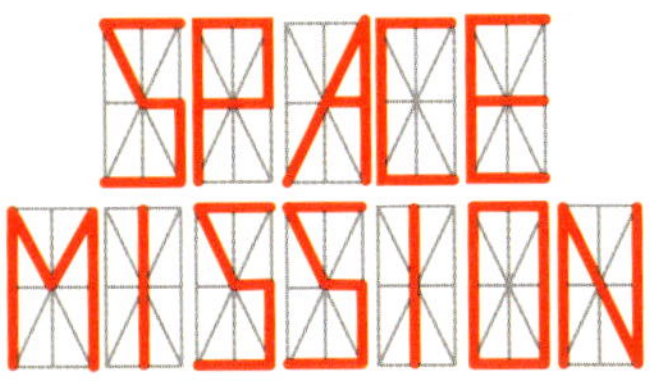

PAGE 55

PAGE 66/67
1. B, 2. D, 3. B, 4. A, 5. C, 6. D, 7. D, 8. B, 9. C, 10. C, 11. D, 12. C

SCIENCE MUSEUM

CONGRATULATIONS YOU MADE IT!

You have now completed your space studies. Fill in your certificate to become an approved Space Explorer.

THIS CERTIFICATE IS AWARDED TO...

....

....

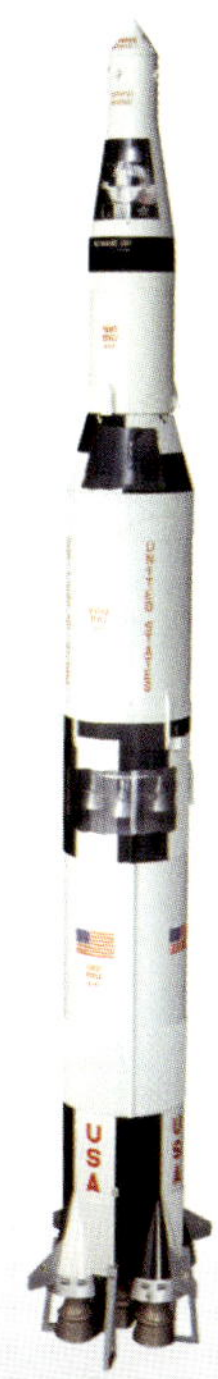

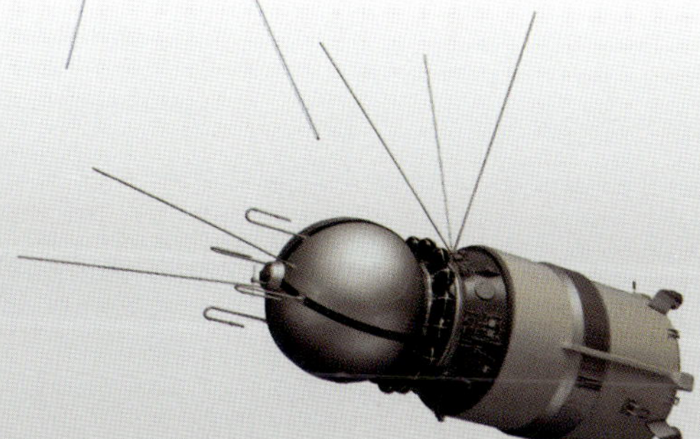

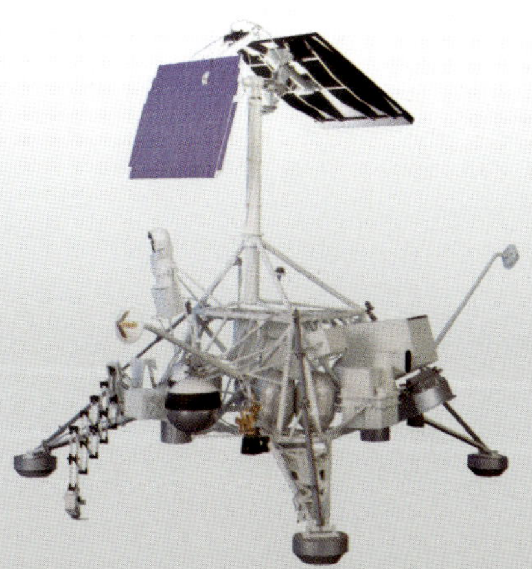